THE TREASURE CHEST

No. 1
Angel of the Battlefield

by Ann Hood
Grosset & Dunlap
An Imprint of Penguin Group (USA) Inc.

GROSSET & DUNLAP
Published by the Penguin Group
Penguin Group (USA) Inc., 375 Hudson Street,
New York, New York 10014, USA
Penguin Group (Canada), 90 Eglinton Avenue East, Suite 700,
Toronto, Ontario M4P 2Y3, Canada
(a division of Pearson Penguin Canada Inc.)
Penguin Books Ltd., 80 Strand, London WC2R 0RL, England
Penguin Group Ireland, 25 St. Stephen's Green, Dublin 2, Ireland
(a division of Penguin Books Ltd.)
Penguin Group (Australia), 250 Camberwell Road, Camberwell, Victoria 3124,
Australia (a division of Pearson Australia Group Pty. Ltd.)
Penguin Books India Pvt. Ltd., 11 Community Centre,
Panchsheel Park, New Delhi—110 017, India
Penguin Group (NZ), 67 Apollo Drive, Rosedale, Auckland 0632, New Zealand
(a division of Pearson New Zealand Ltd.)
Penguin Books (South Africa) (Pty.) Ltd., 24 Sturdee Avenue,
Rosebank, Johannesburg 2196, South Africa

Penguin Books Ltd., Registered Offices: 80 Strand, London WC2R 0RL, England

Text © 2012 by Ann Hood. Illustrations © 2012 by Penguin Group (USA) Inc. Published
by Grosset & Dunlap, a division of Penguin Young Readers Group, 345 Hudson Street,
New York, New York 10014. GROSSET & DUNLAP is a trademark of
Penguin Group (USA) Inc. Printed in the U.S.A.

Cover illustration by Scott Altmann. Map illustration by Meagan Bennett.
Typeset in Mrs Eaves and Adelaide.

Library of Congress Control Number: 2011000846

ISBN 978-0-448-45467-2 (pbk)   10 9 8 7 6 5 4 3 2 1
ISBN 978-0-448-45471-9 (hc)   10 9 8 7 6 5 4 3 2 1

For Virginia Nolan

• CHAPTER ONE •

Newport, Rhode Island

On the hottest day of the hottest summer on record, Maisie and Felix Robbins stood on the rolling front lawn of Elm Medona and wished more than anything that they could go back in time. Five hours ago they had left the apartment at 10 Bethune Street in New York City, where they had lived their entire twelve years, and driven in a U-Haul with their mother to this gigantic, peacock-blue mansion on Bellevue Avenue in Newport, Rhode Island. To Maisie and Felix, it looked more like a museum than a place to live.

"Home, sweet home," their mother said as the three of them stared up at Elm Medona.

Maisie folded her arms across her chest and

glowered at the ridiculous monstrosity their great-great-grandfather Phinneas Pickworth had built in 1909. She would never like living here, she decided. No matter what happened, she would hate it.

Felix, her twin brother, tried not to cry. He was homesick already, and he missed their father, who was having his own moving day halfway across the world.

A horn beeped to announce the arrival of the moving truck.

"Right on time!" their mother said, sprinting across the expansive front lawn to greet the movers.

"What do you think Dad is doing right now?" Felix managed to say. He was a skinny boy and not very tall for twelve, and standing in front of Elm Medona made him feel practically tiny.

"I don't know," Maisie grumbled. On a regular day, her blond curls stuck out of her head like springs. With the heat and humidity, it got even more unruly. She ran her hands over her tangle of hair, trying to tame it a little.

"And I don't care, either," she added, which Felix knew meant she did care. A lot. Maisie might be seven minutes older than Felix was, but he was definitely more mature than her.

Everything in their lives had changed all at once. Or so it seemed to them. Until breakfast one Saturday at the corner diner—Maisie had French toast, Felix a cheese omelet—Maisie and Felix and their parents all lived happily at 10 Bethune Street. But that April morning, their parents told the twins they were getting divorced. *People grow apart*, their mother had said. *They want different things*, their father explained. Those "different things" appeared to be their father taking a job at a big, new museum in Doha, Qatar, and their mother joining a law firm in Newport. *What about us?* Maisie had demanded. Their mother had leaned back in her chair and said, *We get to live in Elm Medona.*

Except they weren't going to live in the mansion. Not exactly. Great-Aunt Maisie, Phinneas Pickworth's daughter, had made an arrangement with the local preservation society years ago. It allowed her to live in the third-floor servants' quarters while the preservation society could give tours of all seventy rooms and eighty acres of it and throw fancy events for wealthy people. Right before that awful morning at the diner, Great-Aunt Maisie had had a stroke and moved into assisted living, leaving the apartment-like attic available for them.

"Aren't we lucky?" their mother said now, pausing to stand beside them. Her own unruly blond hair poked out from a pink bandana she'd tied around her head. She held a box on which she'd written FRAGILE in black Sharpie about a million times.

Maisie and Felix exchanged a look. They had made a vow not to complain to their mother about the terrible twists their lives had taken. *She's going through a lot, too*, Felix had said. *New job. New town. New everything.* Maisie had agreed, reluctantly. *Grown-ups should be able to deal with all this stuff*, she thought. *Especially the grown-ups who made it all happen.*

"So lucky," Maisie said, trying to keep the edge out of her voice.

"At least all of our things have arrived safely," her mother said.

"Do you think there's a pool nearby?" Felix asked as the sun shone down on them through a hazy, humid sky. "Like on Carmine Street?"

"Stop thinking about what *was*," their mother said, "and start thinking about what *is*." With that, she headed through the door with her box.

"It sure is big," Felix said, turning his hazel eyes back to Elm Medona. His square, tortoiseshell glasses slipped down his nose, and he pushed them up.

"It's positively vulgar," Maisie cried. She liked to use vocabulary words whenever possible.

"Can you believe they used to call these things cottages?" Felix said.

He had read the brochure the preservation society had sent them in preparation for their move. It had explained how during the Gilded

Age at the end of the nineteenth century, the tycoons of finance, industry, and mining had built bigger and bigger mansions along Bellevue Avenue. Elm Medona had been the biggest and most lavish of them all. If he didn't have to live there, Felix might have found this information fascinating. Instead, it just gave him a pit in his stomach. He had tried to read the brochure out loud on the drive up, but Maisie made him stop. *I don't care about Elm Medona or the Gilded Age or stupid Phinneas Pickworth!* she'd said miserably.

"I hate Phinneas Pickworth," Maisie said, wiping her sweaty forehead with the back of her hand. "Not only did he build this awful place, but he also fathered Great-Aunt Maisie. And if he hadn't done that, she wouldn't have been able to let us move into this awful place."

Her logic was illogical, but Felix understood. She only meant that she wanted to be back at home on Bethune Street, Rollerblading down the hallway between the apartments and playing softball in Central Park, both of their parents cheering her on.

Felix draped his damp arm around his sister's shoulders. "I hate him, too," he said softly.

Maisie leaned her head on his chest—awkwardly because she was taller than him. The smell of her coconut shampoo mixed with the salty smell of sweat filled his nose.

"There's a gazebo somewhere on the grounds," Felix offered hopefully. *Gazebo* was a good vocabulary word, too. Maybe that would win her over.

Maisie sighed.

"Phinneas copied it from a famous French temple called the Temple of Love," Felix added.

Maisie glanced up at him. Even though they were twins, they looked nothing alike. Maisie had inherited everything from their mother—unruly blond hair, big, green eyes, long legs—and Felix had inherited everything from their father—hazel eyes flecked with gold and afflicted with nearsightedness, stick-straight, brown hair, and even the cowlick that refused to be tamed.

She turned those green eyes on him now and said, "I want to go back. I want to close my eyes, and when I open them again, I want to be in our room on Bethune Street with Mom and Dad both in the kitchen, laughing and singing show tunes."

"Me too," Felix said, giving her a squeeze. "But there's no going back." Saying that gave him a big lump in his throat. He swallowed hard three times, trying to make it go away.

For most of their childhood, their mother had been an actress, going to auditions and taking voice and dance lessons and scene-study classes; their father had been a sculptor, working in a big studio downtown that he rode his bike to every morning after he dropped them off at school. But a few years ago, their mother had gone to law school, and their father had taken a job in an art gallery. *Maybe*, Felix thought, *that was when everything started to change.*

From high above them, their mother pushed open a window and popped her head out. "Are you just going to stand there all day, or are you going to help unpack some boxes?"

"We're going to explore!" Maisie shouted back.

"Don't go too far," their mother said. "And make sure you can find your way back."

Felix laughed. "Not everybody has a backyard as big as eighty football fields where they can actually get lost," he said. "With real temples and English gardens and who knows what else."

"Isn't there a carriage house with a bunch of old cars in it?" Maisie said.

Felix pointed a finger at her. "Aha! You *were* listening."

"Reluctantly," she said, peering off into the distance where the grounds seemed to go on forever. "I see something way down there," she said.

Without hesitating, Maisie walked off. As usual, Felix had to hurry to catch up with her.

Later, Felix and Maisie entered Elm Medona through a side door off a circular driveway practically hidden by trees and high hedges. It was the same door the servants and deliverymen used to use. Inside, no one would ever guess they were in a mansion. The small vestibule had a worn linoleum floor and a plain wooden staircase. One flight down was the mansion's enormous kitchen. And three flights up were the servants' quarters—which Maisie and Felix would now call home.

"This is depressing," Maisie said as they climbed the stairs. With each flight they climbed, the staircase grew narrower and steeper.

Felix didn't answer. Once again, homesickness swept over him.

At the top, the door flew open and their mother came out, her big polka-dot purse slung over her shoulder and her blond hair pulled into a ponytail.

"It's as hot as Hades in there," she warned them. "No way am I turning on the stove. Start unpacking while I grab us some sandwich stuff."

"You'll be right back, right?" Felix asked her as she hurried past them.

"See if you can find the fan," their mother called over her shoulder.

When Maisie and Felix walked into the apartment, Felix groaned. It was hotter inside than outside, the walls were painted a depressing, dull yellow, and he could smell the distinct odor of old lady.

"It's not bad," Maisie said, just so her brother would feel better.

Truthfully, it was worse than bad. She walked through the small kitchen into an equally small living room. Their boxes stood stacked against the walls. The windows were tiny and smudged, the floors were old and scuffed, and nothing about it seemed like home. The living room opened onto a long, dark hallway with bedrooms lining each side and a bathroom all the way at the end. It had a big claw-foot tub and a tiled floor with funny pictures of goats and bulls and fish.

When Maisie opened one bedroom door she saw a small, square room with two twin beds, a bureau, and a rocking chair. She opened the door across the hall to reveal an identical room. The next room was the same. And the next.

"Boy," Felix said, trying to imagine all the

people who used to live there a long time ago. "Phinneas Pickworth had a lot of servants."

"Well," she said to Felix, "which room do you want? Not that it matters since they're all the same."

"The one across the hall from yours," Felix said.

Maisie pointed to the first room she'd looked at. "I'll take that one then," she said.

"Okay," Felix said. "I guess we should start unpacking."

"We're going to die of heat exhaustion," Maisie said as she went back into the living room to find the boxes with her name written on them.

"I'll get us some water," Felix said.

In the kitchen, he tried to find glasses in the cupboards, but they were all empty. Then he saw it: a door that opened into a tall, narrow elevator.

"You've got to see this!" he called to his sister.

Maisie came over and peered inside. She tried to squeeze in, but Felix yanked her out.

"You're no fun," she said. "Hey, I know! Let's go see what the rest of the house looks like."

"I don't think we're supposed to do that," Felix told her.

"Says who?"

He thought for a minute. No one had actually told them they couldn't go downstairs, but it had been made clear that they lived on the *third floor*, and the rest of the house belonged to the preservation society.

"We're getting a tour on Monday," Felix reminded Maisie.

"Monday is a million years from now," Maisie said.

He would have reminded her that Monday was Labor Day and the mansion was closed to the public so they would be getting a private VIP tour, but she went out the kitchen door, into the hallway, and down the steps. Felix rushed out behind her.

On the first landing, Maisie paused in front of the door. Felix came beside her and looked out the window. Down below he could see the circular driveway, mostly hidden by foliage.

Maisie grunted. "Locked," she said, disappointed as she tugged on the door. Immediately she turned and continued down the stairs to the next landing.

Surely something interesting lies beyond these doors, she thought. Like when she stepped outside their apartment building on Bethune Street, she always saw something new. Once she had seen a man walking a rabbit on a leash, and she had followed him all the way to the Bleecker Street Playground. Another time, she had practically walked right into Lance Armstrong, and she had stayed beside him until he had ducked into the French bistro up the street. Who knew what she might find behind one of these doors.

"Locked!" she cried as she tried the next door.

"Clearly," Felix said, "they don't want anyone going inside."

Maisie ignored him. She placed her hip against the door and gave a good, hard shove. The door didn't budge.

"Aaarrgghhh," she cried, frustrated.

"They have to keep it locked, Maisie," Felix said. "There must be millions of dollars worth of valuable stuff in there." When she didn't answer him and just kept pushing against the door with not only her hip but her shoulder and both hands, too, he added, "Maybe even billions of dollars worth."

Maisie stopped pushing long enough to say, "Don't be dumb." Then she threw her whole body at the door as if her life depended on getting inside.

The door sighed softly. It shuddered as if it might open. But it remained closed.

"Maybe if we both try?" Maisie asked.

If he said no, Felix knew she would pester him until he said yes.

"Okay," Felix said in a voice that let her know he didn't really want to do this.

The two of them stepped back, leaned their

shoulders forward, and hurled themselves at the stubborn door.

Another sigh. But this time it budged ever so slightly.

"It's probably just a sitting room or something," Felix said, rubbing his shoulder. "Not very interesting."

Maisie frowned at the door.

"I'm starving," Felix said, thinking of a turkey sandwich with American cheese. "We haven't eaten since we stopped in Connecticut on the way here. And that was hours ago."

Maisie ignored him. She bent and inspected the lock, fiddled with the knob, and then stepped back again.

"I bet she'll get that ham you like," he said, trying to get his sister to go back upstairs.

She brightened. "We need a ruler," she said. "I'll push, and when it opens a crack, you can stick the ruler in and, I don't know, pop the lock."

"In the movies, robbers use credit cards," Felix said. His stomach grumbled.

"Even better!" she said. "We'll wait till Mom goes to sleep, and then you can sneak into her wallet—"

"Me?" Felix said.

"Well, why do I have to do everything?" Maisie asked.

"But I don't even care what's in there. And even if I did, I'm going to find out in two days when we get our tour," Felix responded.

They glared at each other.

The stairway felt like it had no air at all.

"Maybe she'll get lemonade," Felix said hopefully.

"She did get lemonade," their mother said, appearing on the stairway below them. "Are you two snooping around?"

"We're not," Felix answered.

Their mother's flip-flops shuffled up the stairs until she loomed in front of them, her arms full of grocery bags. Her ponytail drooped, and her face glistened with sweat.

"Upstairs," she said, handing each of them a bag. "Now."

"But it's so boring—" Maisie began.

"You have been here all of what? A few hours?" their mother said, stepping aside and waving her one free arm for them to get moving. "You haven't had time to get bored."

Felix gave her a big smile when he walked past her, but she did not smile back.

"How am I going to trust you two when I start work on Tuesday?" their mother said as they climbed up, single file. "This is a new job that I

wouldn't even have if I wasn't Phinneas Pickwi
great-granddaughter. Do you think law firms
Newport, Rhode Island, are desperate for lawyers?
They are not," she answered before they could. "I
have to prove myself, you know, and not worry that
you two are going to get into all kinds of trouble."

"I didn't know we had to stay locked up all day
like Rapunzel or somebody," Maisie said.

When they reached the top of the stairs and the
door to their apartment, their mother turned to
face them. The heat had made her mascara melt
and leave black smudges around her eyes so she
resembled a raccoon.

"This is hard," she said. "Hard, hard, hard.
But we have to put one foot in front of the other.
All of us do." For an instant it looked as though
she might cry. But she took a deep breath and
collected herself. "There are eighty acres of
grounds out there," she said. "You can spend the
next six days until school starts exploring them."

She opened the door to their tiny, hot
apartment.

"Your great-great-grandfather was an
explorer, you know," she said, unpacking the
shopping bags.

Felix smiled as he watched her take out turkey
and a package of American cheese.

"Why, he sailed down the Nile," she continued, "and visited the tombs of Queen Hatshepsut and—"

Maisie watched her unpack, too. "I bet they don't even have the ham I like here," Maisie said miserably.

"They do," their mother said. She held up a neatly wrapped package of deli meat. "See? We're not exactly in the middle of nowhere."

That was when Felix told his mother about the gazebo. He thought it might make her happy that they had indeed explored a little.

"The inside ceiling is painted light blue with clouds," he said. "And there's a little bench in there with the back shaped like a heart."

"Phinneas Pickworth was a romantic." Their mother sighed.

After they finished their sandwiches and potato chips—barbecue for Maisie, ripples for Felix—their mother brought out a pound cake.

"Let them eat cake," she said.

They looked at her, puzzled.

"That's Marie Antoinette's most famous line," their mother told them. "She said it when—"

"Mom, who cares what some lady who died a million years ago said?" Maisie asked.

Their mother sighed again. "It wouldn't hurt you to learn a little something about history and people you've never heard of."

"Mom?" Felix said, his mouth full of cake.

"Swallow first," she said.

Felix swallowed. "Why aren't we allowed in the mansion? I mean, isn't it technically ours?"

She shook her head. "It belongs to the preservation society. As long as heirs of Phinneas Pickworth are alive, they can rent this apartment for a dollar a year."

"A dollar?" Maisie gasped. "For this whole place?"

"The money is kind of symbolic. That's the agreement Great-Aunt Maisie made when she couldn't afford the upkeep on Elm Medona any longer."

"Why didn't she just sell it?" Maisie asked.

"It's where she lived her whole life," their mother said. She collected the paper plates and wiped the crumbs from the table onto them. "You should hear her stories about growing up in this place. Her father built it as a summer cottage, but the family liked it so much they ended up living here full time. She and her twin brother used to slide down the Grand Staircase and hold tea parties on the lawn."

"Great-Aunt Maisie is a twin?" Maisie said, surprised.

"You have more in common with your namesake

than you thought." Their mother grinned. "She has a twin brother, Thorne, who lives in London. Growing up, they used to be as close . . . well, as close as you two. According to Great-Aunt Maisie, they had adventures like no one else. Adventures they could have only at Elm Medona. She seems to believe there's something so special about this place that she can't let it go."

Maisie shook her head. "I can't imagine anything that special here."

"Wait until you get the VIP tour," their mother said. "Maybe you'll change your mind."

"Don't count on it," Maisie said, cutting another piece of pound cake.

"Maybe we're in for a big surprise," Felix said.

He said it to make his mother feel better. But secretly he hoped something amazing did lay in store for them in Elm Medona.

• CHAPTER TWO •

The Woman in Pink

On Monday morning, Felix felt his mother kiss him good-bye. Or maybe he dreamed it. But either way, when he got out of bed, she was gone, and a note lay on the kitchen table that said: *Have a great day! I'll be at work setting up my office! Enjoy the tour and stay out of trouble!!! Love, Mom.* A giant box of cereal and two bananas sat on top of the note. Felix took a paper plate from the counter, cut himself a big piece of leftover pound cake, and poured a paper cup full of milk. Over the weekend, his mother had unpacked all the real dishes and glasses and carefully arranged them in the cupboard, but if he used something, he would have to wash it himself. Unlike their apartment in New York, there was no dishwasher here.

He had already finished his first piece of cake and was working his way through half of a second one when Maisie walked into the kitchen. She didn't bother getting a plate. She just cut a piece of pound cake and bit into it, letting crumbs fall everywhere.

Outside, thunder rumbled.

"Great," Maisie said. "It's going to rain, and we'll be stuck inside forever."

"We have the tour today, anyway," Felix reminded her.

The phone rang, startling them. They'd lived here three whole days, and the phone had not rung even once.

"Hello?" Felix said tentatively.

His father's voice said, "Felix? Felix?"

"Dad!" Felix shouted.

Immediately Maisie tried to pull the phone away from him. "Dad!" she yelled.

Felix turned the receiver so they could both talk and listen.

"How's Newport?" their father asked. "How's Elm Medona?"

"Hot," Felix said.

"Boring," Maisie said.

"Sounds like Doha." Their father laughed.

"Maybe you should come—" Felix stopped

himself. He almost said *home*, but where was that exactly? "Back," he finished.

"Well, the museum is great," their father said. "And I like the job a lot. I just miss you guys, and hot dogs and—"

"Mom?" Maisie said.

"Like I said. I miss you guys," their father said softly. "But once you get your computers going, we'll set up Skype and—"

"We can't get Internet here," Maisie said. "Something about the walls."

"Oh," he said, disappointed. "Well, I'll be back at Christmas, and that's practically around the corner."

Felix and Maisie knew Christmas was far off, but they both mumbled, "Sure."

"I love you, guys," their father said.

He had his hanging-up voice on now, and Felix wanted to shout for him not to.

"Love you, too," Felix said.

Then came the sound of hanging up and the eerie silence of disconnection.

The clock on the stove said 9:24. Maisie tried not to think about what she would be doing on Bethune Street right now.

"You know," she said, "adults always tell us we can have anything we want if we just work hard and try our best. But all I want is to turn that clock back to . . . to . . . 9:24 AM last year or . . . or . . . any year really that was happier than this one. And that's the one thing I can't have."

Felix couldn't remember exactly what he had been doing a year ago, but he agreed with Maisie. Whatever it was, he had certainly been happier then.

"I guess they just mean we can become doctors or astronauts or something," he said. "Possible things."

"Well, I don't care," Maisie said. "I want an impossible thing."

As if this were all his fault, she stomped out of the kitchen, dropping crumbs behind her.

"Hey!" Felix called. "What's that? A trail to find your way back?"

"Ha-ha," Maisie said and slammed her bedroom door shut.

At precisely noon, a lady wearing pink— lipstick, scarf, nail polish, too tight sweater— met them outside at the main entrance to Elm Medona for what she called a Grand-VIP-Private- Behind-the-Scenes Tour. She twittered like a bird with excitement about Elm Medona. People came from miles away just to examine its marble and wallpaper, she told them.

"What lucky children you are," the Woman in Pink chirped, "to live in a piece of history like Elm Medona."

"So we've been told," Maisie muttered.

The Woman in Pink cleared her throat. "Well," she said. "I believe that by the end of this tour you will agree with the general consensus."

The thunder that had stayed off in the distance suddenly grew nearer. A loud clap burst through the sky, and the wind picked up, whistling eerily and shaking the branches of the large oak trees that lined the driveway leading to where they stood.

All three of them glanced heavenward. The wind grew stronger. The Woman in Pink had to raise her voice to be heard above it.

"Well, shall we begin? I've been a docent for the preservation society since 1998—"

"A what?" Maisie said.

"A *docent*. A tour guide of sorts. For museums and the like. Now, as you may know—"

"Docent," Maisie said under her breath. "*D . . . o . . . s*—"

"*C*," the Woman in Pink said impatiently. "*D-o-c-e-n-t*. Now where was I?"

"You've been a docent since 1998," Felix reminded her.

The Woman in Pink closed her eyes briefly as if to collect her thoughts. When she opened them, she said in a measured voice, "As you may know, Phinneas Pickworth built Elm Medona in 1909 as a summer cottage for his wife, Ariane. Ariane Pickworth was from French royalty, and, in fact, Phinneas met her in Paris . . ."

Maisie got bored immediately. But Felix didn't. Phinneas Pickworth sounded like someone out of an adventure story. Felix was thrilled at the thought that he shared Phinneas's DNA. Truth be told, Felix was a worrywart, a bit shy, and—as Maisie liked to say—afraid of his own shadow. He got in trouble only when he let Maisie talk him into doing something wrong. Teachers liked him for his enthusiasm for reading and the way he volunteered to wash down the chalkboards and put the chairs up on the desks on Fridays. Parents liked him because he remembered to say please and thank you. Yet a relative of his had sailed the Nile and climbed the Great Wall of China. Things Felix never imagined he would ever do.

"And such a shame that Ariane died giving birth," the Woman in Pink was saying, "having spent only two summers in Elm Medona. Her portrait hangs above the green marble fireplace in the Drawing Room." She lowered her voice as if she were about to share a secret. "That fireplace is an exact replica of a fireplace in Versailles."

Again, the wind blew loud and hard, tossing Maisie's hair into her face.

"My goodness," the Woman in Pink said, opening the massive front doors. "The weather report said nothing at all about a storm."

As if to disprove that, lightning flashed across the sky, which had gone from blue to gray while they stood outside.

"We'd better get inside," she said, waving her arms at them.

Maisie and Felix walked into the enormous foyer, and both of them gasped. Never had they stood in a place so grand. Not even the Metropolitan Museum of Art or the American Museum of Natural History. They didn't know where to look first. At the soaring ceiling painted with pink clouds and dancing nymphs? At the Grand Staircase that swooped and rose majestically upward? At the beautiful, stained-glass window above it? Through the back wall of giant windows at the ocean, which wildly tossed enormous gray waves topped with whitecaps? Felix glimpsed one room whose walls appeared to be made of red leather and another that glistened with what might be real gold.

"Each one of these doors weighs one and a half tons, roughly the weight of a rhinoceros," the Woman in Pink recited. She pointed at a carved face. "That's Apollo, the god of the sun—Louis XIV's personal symbol."

The foyer darkened as booming thunder, followed by more crackling lightning, erupted. Rain splashed against the stained-glass windows, hard and fast.

The Woman in Pink frowned. "My goodness," she said. "How strange. I'm certain the weatherman called for another hot, sunny day."

Felix noticed that, despite the warmth of the house and the pink sweater the woman wore, she shivered.

"Elm Medona," she said softly.

"What about it?" Maisie asked, studying the woman's face carefully.

"People say strange things go on here," the Woman in Pink said.

"Like ghosts and stuff?" Felix asked, worried.

Just then came the sound of something falling upstairs, and a loud crash reverberated through the house.

The Woman in Pink said, "Oh! Dear!" She ran across the marble floor and up the Grand Staircase.

Maisie took off after her, calling to Felix over her shoulder, "Come on! This might be an actual ghost!"

"Exactly," Felix said, pressing himself against the sturdy door. "That's why I'm staying right here."

At the top of the stairs, Maisie bumped smack into the Woman in Pink, already on her way back down.

"I have to call the preservation society," the woman said, taking a pink cell phone from her bag. Her hands trembled as she punched in the numbers. "One of the Ming vases broke."

Maisie peered past the Woman in Pink and saw shards of blue-and-white porcelain scattered across the rug.

The rain beat down harder still, and the sound of the wind grew even louder.

"Hello? Hello?" the Woman in Pink shouted into the phone. Her panicked eyes met Maisie's. "I lost them," she said. She glanced at the phone in her still-trembling hand. "I don't have a signal anymore."

"Do you think it's Phinneas Pickworth's ghost?" Maisie asked hopefully. "Do you think he's causing all this trouble?"

"Don't be silly," the Woman in Pink said, forcing a laugh. "There's no such thing as ghosts."

By that phony laugh and the way the Woman in Pink looked away from her, Maisie could tell she didn't believe that.

"Has anyone seen his ghost?" Maisie said in a whisper.

"Well, some people swear they've seen a man with a big handlebar mustache dressed in explorer's gear up here. And some claim they've seen Ariane's ghost in the nursery, but surely that's just a case of overactive imaginations," the Woman in Pink said unconvincingly.

"Maisie?" Felix asked from below.

"It's nothing!" Maisie yelled. "Just a fancy vase."

"A *priceless* fancy vase," the Woman in Pink said as she tried to call the preservation society again.

"Well," Felix said, "are you coming back down?"

The Woman in Pink snapped her phone shut. "Yes," she said. "Let's just continue with the tour."

She took a deep breath, straightened her shoulders, and began down the stairway. Disappointed, Maisie hesitated. With the Woman in Pink out of the way, she could see that the pieces of the broken vase lay in an almost-straight line. She had broken enough glasses to know that the shards didn't fall neatly. They scattered. Everywhere.

How peculiar, Maisie thought. She remembered what Felix had said just this morning when she'd spilled pound cake crumbs. *A trail to find your way back.* Was someone—or something—trying to find its way back here? But that didn't quite make sense. Whatever caused all this ruckus was already here, wasn't it? *Maybe,* Maisie thought—and she grew excited at the very idea—*maybe this trail leads to something. Maybe it is intended to lead me to something.*

She could hear the Woman in Pink downstairs exclaiming about the Dining Room. "Why, it is considered the most beautiful dining room in the world!" she gushed.

Maisie walked over to the broken vase. She swore the pieces glistened despite the darkness from the storm. But to her utter disappointment, the line of shards led to nothing except an ordinary wall—if a wall covered in some kind of lush green fabric could be called ordinary. Maisie ran her hand over the wall as if she might find something surprising there. But all she felt was the smooth fabric and the hard wood underneath it. She could hear Felix, and although she couldn't make out the words, from the rise and fall of his voice, Maisie knew he was asking questions. Millions of them. She sighed. For a moment it had seemed that something special was indeed about to happen. But there was nothing up here except a broken vase.

Maisie turned to go back downstairs and hear every boring detail about the Dining Room when she paused. *No one had said anything about not taking a little souvenir*, she thought. Maisie surveyed the pieces, wanting to choose the best one. But there was another weird thing: Every piece was identical. Same size. Same shape. And Maisie knew that when things broke, they didn't break so neatly.

Bending to inspect them closer, Maisie also saw that each piece had one perfect blue flower on it. The break had not disrupted the pattern. Curious, she picked up a random shard. The porcelain was smooth—even at the sides, which, she knew, should have been rough from breaking apart. The porcelain seemed to hum in her hand.

That was when she realized how silent the house had grown.

Sunlight streamed through the stained-glass windows decorated with half-naked dancing gods and goddesses. The storm had ended as abruptly as it had begun.

The Woman in Pink's voice cut through the quiet as she returned to the foyer. "The bronze dining chairs are so heavy they required four servants to move them—diners couldn't do it on their own."

"Wow," Felix said.

"Next, we'll visit Ariane Pickworth's library, where the walls are made of pink marble imported from Italy . . . but where has that sister of yours gone?"

"Here!" Maisie called, sticking the shard into her pocket.

She practically skipped down the stairs, where Felix and the Woman in Pink both stood waiting for her with worried expressions on their faces. Maisie tried to give Felix a look that told him she had something exciting to share, but he refused to make eye contact with her. Instead, he trailed right behind the Woman in Pink as she talked about rare books and the Muses from Greek mythology and dead Ariane Pickworth.

•CHAPTER THREE•

The Treasure Chest

The Woman in Pink droned on about fireplaces sent over from France and how many hours it had taken to sew the beads on their great-grandmother's wedding dress. Maisie smiled and nodded politely. All while the Woman in Pink talked about industrialists and income taxes and the growth of the city of Newport, Maisie kept her hand in her pocket, feeling the slight bump of porcelain there.

Perhaps the most boring part of the entire tour was the Kitchen, which was down a dark flight of stairs off the Dining Room. As if seeing some out-of-use kitchen wasn't dull enough, the Woman in Pink had one last thing to show them.

She ushered them toward a dimly lit stairway in the corner. Once down the stairs, they found themselves in a small, freezing-cold room.

"It's like a freezer in here," Felix said, shivering.

"Phinneas Pickworth was clever!" she said. "Refrigeration before it was even invented!"

She explained in excruciating detail how he devised a way to make ice and how he had coal brought into another part of this subbasement by a little underground train—just so his family and guests didn't see it being delivered.

"Phinneas Pickworth thought of everything," she said with an adoring sigh. Maisie was starting to hate Phinneas Pickworth.

They stood forever in front of a complicated board that looked like the flight-departure board at an airport but really was just a system for calling servants with little, yellow lights and lots of wires and numbers.

"I think I'm actually dying of boredom," Maisie whispered to Felix.

The Woman in Pink frowned at them. "So," she said finally, "I think that just about covers the Kitchen."

"Wow," Maisie said, "this was fascinating." She grabbed Felix's arm and nudged him toward the stairs.

"Yeah," he said. "Really amazing."

"Oh!" the Woman in Pink said, tapping her temple. "I almost forgot."

Maisie groaned.

The woman walked over to a small, narrow door and opened it. Reluctantly, they followed her.

"The first elevator?" Felix asked politely.

The Woman in Pink laughed. "Oh, dear, no. It's a dumbwaiter."

Maisie stepped inside. "It looks like an elevator," she said. "Like the one we have upstairs."

"Could you step out, please? It isn't part of the tour to actually go inside the dumbwaiter."

"What's a dumbwaiter?" Felix asked.

"It was used to ferry things from the Kitchen to all the floors and then back down. Imagine all the time they saved, sending the tea service up to Ariane's room in the morning. Or the turkeys and hams and roast beefs to the Dining Room."

The Woman in Pink explained the mechanics of how the dumbwaiter worked. She talked about pulleys and square footage while Maisie stayed inside, staring upward.

"Just how far up does this thing go?" she interrupted.

The woman *tsk-tsked*. "As I was saying, it goes

all the way up to the servants' quarters . . . I
mean, to your apartment."

"That *is* what we have in the kitchen!" Felix said.

"Shall we continue?" the woman said,
looking directly at Maisie. "Since being *inside* the
dumbwaiter is off-limits."

The Woman in Pink's favorite phrase was
"off-limits," as in "this bedroom is *off-limits*" and
"that hallway is *off-limits*." Maisie especially liked
peering into all those off-limit rooms, which
looked exactly like the boring ones they could
enter except that a red velvet rope hung across the
doorway. A fancy way to say "keep out."

Maisie left the dumbwaiter, and she and Felix
followed the Woman in Pink back up the stairs
and through the Dining Room where a giant
wooden table was set with Phinneas Pickworth's
china. The Woman in Pink explained that the
china had its very own pattern designed just for
Phinneas by some famous person—alternating
peacocks and pineapples along the rim and a big
pair of interlocking *P*s in the center—all of it laid
out as if Phinneas himself was about to host a
dinner party. Felix thought it was kind of creepy
to leave the table set like that.

Out they went into yet another room, this one
circular.

"The Grand Ballroom was considered the heart of the house," the Woman in Pink was saying. Her hands swept upward. "It was the first room in the United States to incorporate lattice design as a decorative scheme."

"Ah," Felix said, just to say something.

Up the Grand Staircase they went, the Woman in Pink describing the statues, the tapestries, and the marble banisters. Every inch of the place had a story behind it. Felix tried to imagine Great-Aunt Maisie as a young girl. To him, she was the shriveled old lady they'd been forced to visit twice over the weekend in the nursing home, who ate cottage cheese and had a crooked mouth and talked all garbled. It was hard—almost impossible—for him to imagine her ever being his age.

The Woman in Pink paused briefly at a black-and-white photograph that hung on the wall.

"Here's someone you know quite well," she said.

Felix stared right into the eyes of the little girl in the picture. "Great-Aunt Maisie?" he said softly.

"That's correct," she said and continued up the stairs.

But Felix stayed put, studying the soft, pretty face of the little girl. She had braids and wore a white dress. Behind her, it looked like a party was taking place, with blurry people in fancy clothes on the great lawn that rolled down to the ocean. Felix pressed his finger against the glass as if he could actually touch the little girl. Could this really be the same person who lay all wrinkled and infirmed in that assisted living place? The thought made him sad for reasons he couldn't explain.

Felix leaned closer to the picture. At the edge of the photograph a little boy peeked out as if he'd run into the field of the camera's eye at the very last moment.

"Who's the boy in the picture?" Felix asked.

"Thorne Pickworth," the Woman in Pink said. "Maisie's twin brother."

Both Thorne and Maisie had a twinkle in their eyes, like kids who had a secret.

The Woman in Pink cleared her throat. "We're going upstairs now, Felix," she said. "We're already running late here."

Reluctantly, Felix continued up the stairway, feeling as if those two kids in that photograph were watching him.

"Now here's something special that Elm Medona has," the Woman in Pink said when Felix reached the hallway at the top of the Grand Staircase. "Something children like very much."

Maisie stared. She blinked her eyes. She blinked again.

"The—the vase," she stammered.

"What vase?" the Woman in Pink said.

"The priceless one," Maisie said, pointing. "The *broken*, priceless one."

All three of them stared at the lush rug—which the Woman in Pink had said was handwoven by a blind family in Persia. But there was nothing there except the rug's intricate pattern of birds and vines. Not one piece of porcelain remained as if it had all been swept up and put away.

"How strange," the Woman in Pink said. She went right to the spot where the shards had been and dropped to her knees, running her hands carefully over the carpet. "Maybe the cleaning staff . . . ," she began, but trailed off.

"Was there really something broken there?" Felix asked in a small voice.

The Woman in Pink stood, smoothing her pink skirt. "Obviously the preservation society got my message and sent the cleaners over. Why, they're probably trying to piece it back together as we speak."

Maisie placed her hand in her pocket and fingered the smooth shard there.

"So. Where were we? Ah, yes. As you may know," the Woman in Pink trilled, "Phinneas Pickworth was a rascal. He was an adventurer, a collector, a lover of magic and practical jokes."

The Woman in Pink touched the wall with the special French Louis-the-somebody's green-and-gold paneling. It was the very spot where Maisie had hoped to find something extraordinary when the vase broke. Like magic, the wall opened to reveal a staircase.

"What in the world . . . ?" Maisie said, jumping back slightly.

Felix gasped. "A hidden stairway!"

"Oh!" Maisie said. "This is absolutely incredible!"

"Maybe the coolest thing ever," Felix said.

"Where did the wall go?" Maisie said, running her fingers along the edges where the wall had just been. That broken vase *had* left a trail, right to here. Something special waited at the top of those stairs, Maisie was certain of it.

"As you can see, this section of the wall spins into this recessed part here," the Woman in Pink began to explain.

Without hesitating, Maisie started up the stairs.

"No, no, no! The Treasure Chest is *off-limits*," the Woman in Pink said in her fluttery voice, teetering after Maisie in her pink high heels.

That really piqued Maisie's interest. "The Treasure Chest?" she said, stopping midway up. "Is that what's up here?"

Maisie didn't wait for an answer. Treasure

chests held gold and jewels and all sorts of interesting things. She quickly climbed up the rest of the stairs, disappearing at the top.

"Oh, dear," the Woman in Pink said. She looked helplessly at Felix. "The Treasure Chest is most absolutely off-limits."

Felix nodded at her, his stomach sinking with every syllable she spoke. *Off-limits* was just fine with him. Now the Woman in Pink disappeared upstairs, too. With a sigh, Felix followed.

At the top, Maisie stood with her body pressed against the red velvet rope that stretched across the doorway of a large room filled floor to ceiling with . . . more stuff than Felix had ever seen all in one place. He blinked, trying to take in what he was looking at.

"What is all this stuff?" he asked.

Peacock feathers jutted from carved wooden boxes. Seashells lay on weathered bones. Test tubes shone beside parchment paper, which rested on top of faded fabric that partially covered a chest of old tools nestled beside pieces of jade. And that was just what he saw at first glance. The harder he stared, the more objects he could make out: maps and bows and a compass and a wheel of some kind; antlers and maybe real jewels and an inkwell with a feathered pen in it and—

"How can this be?" Maisie said, startled.

She pushed Felix aside and started to unhook the rope. Right there, in the middle of all that stuff, on an ornately carved pedestal, sat a huge blue-and-white porcelain vase.

But the Woman in Pink grabbed her elbow and yanked her away.

"*Off-limits*," she chirped—nervously, Maisie thought.

"But that vase *broke!*" Maisie said, pointing. "Not even an hour ago!"

"No, no," the Woman in Pink said uncertainly. "As I said, your great-great-grandfather was a collector. He must have acquired a set of Mings. A matching pair." She began to flip the pages on her clipboard, searching for something. "There's a list in here of the valuable pieces . . . ," she muttered.

Maisie squinted at the vase before her, fingering the shard she'd pocketed.

"It's the same one!" she blurted. Right there in the middle, Maisie saw a missing piece. *Her* piece.

"That is impossible," the Woman in Pink said. But she didn't look like she believed that it was impossible. In fact, she looked up from her papers and stared at the vase, too.

"How do you know?" Felix said to his sister. He pushed his glasses up higher on his nose.

"Just trust me," Maisie said. "I know."

"I think we are all being a little dramatic," the Woman in Pink said. "Phinneas Pickworth collected so many treasures that they aren't even all catalogued properly. Just look at all of it! You can see why they call this room The Treasure Chest."

"I'll say," Felix said. "I've never seen so much stuff in my life. Not even at the American Museum of Natural History."

Felix joined Maisie at the entrance to the room and peered in.

"Young man! Step back! This room isn't even part of the tour." The Woman in Pink's face flushed as pink as her lipstick. In a shaky voice she added, "You have no idea what has gone on in here."

"Is it haunted?" Felix asked, stepping back.

"No such thing," Maisie muttered.

"Exactly!" the Woman in Pink said. "Of course, all of these old houses have their share of unexplained phenomena. And Elm Medona goes far beyond the usual reports of transparent women floating down the stairs and strange noises. Why, they say that in this very room—" She stopped suddenly as if she had just realized that she was talking to children. "But as I said, it's probably hogwash."

She began to walk away, motioning for them to follow.

"Now, down the hall is the nursery, which I think you'll find most fascinating."

Maisie hesitated, peeking again into The Treasure Chest. That vase had been broken less than an hour ago. Now it stood in The Treasure Chest, put back together. Except for one piece. And that piece was in Maisie's pocket. *Off-limits?* Maisie grinned. She would figure out a way to get inside that room. Soon.

· CHAPTER FOUR ·

Breaking In

For some reason, Maisie and Felix both thought the tour was a way to show them around their new home. But as soon as it was over, the Woman in Pink said, "If you ever want to come back in the cottage proper, your mother just has to make an appointment."

"An appointment?" Maisie said.

The Woman in Pink smiled nervously. She had a smear of pink lipstick on her front teeth, and the buttons on her pink suit jacket pulled in awkward directions. "Your family stays right upstairs in the family quarters. Like your great-aunt did for so long."

Despite a childhood in Elm Medona with

tea parties in the gazebo and croquet games on the rolling lawn, Great-Aunt Maisie had spent practically her whole adult life stuck up on the third floor. Once a year, she visited them in New York City and insisted on taking them to the Metropolitan Museum of Art, where she went to the Temple of Dendur and murmured about King Tut like he was an old friend. Or she brought them to the Museum of Modern Art where she stood in front of Van Gogh's painting, muttering *Vincent, Vincent.*

Felix thought she was sad, but Maisie thought she was a little crazy. *Just because I'm named after her doesn't mean I have to like her,* Maisie had told him.

"Your great-aunt certainly led an interesting life," the Woman in Pink said, and something in the way she said it made Maisie suspicious.

"How interesting can it be to be locked upstairs?" Maisie said.

Felix looked up. "Like prisoners," he said.

"Not at all," the Woman in Pink said, fiddling with her scarf. "Like guests."

Maisie watched her fiddling.

"What exactly went on in The Treasure Chest?" Maisie asked. "Do you think Phinneas Pickworth is haunting it? Haunting the whole house maybe?"

"No, no. There are so many stories about Elm Medona. Why, some people believe that your great-aunt and her brother, Thorne—" She stopped abruptly.

"That they what?" Maisie asked.

The Woman in Pink sighed. "Such lucky children," she said. "Living among history."

Felix thought about Bleecker Street Playground, where he and Maisie had played together forever, and the long corridor in their apartment building where they rode their bikes on rainy days. He did not feel lucky at all. He just felt homesick.

"Off with you now," the Woman in Pink said, shooing them away like they were nothing more than flies.

She opened a door in the Dining Room that led to the narrow servants' stairway and their apartment.

"Thank you for the tour," Felix remembered to say.

The Woman in Pink wiggled her fingers at them, then closed the door firmly.

Maisie and Felix stood at the bottom of the stairs for a few moments and pondered the rules of their new "home." They weren't allowed to play on the lawn until the last tour ended—and then only if an event wasn't scheduled for that night. There was also a big calendar of mansion events that hung over their kitchen table. It was the only thing their mother had had time to hang up.

"I hate it here," Maisie said.

"So do I," Felix said.

"Nothing to do," Maisie said, starting up the stairs.

"Nowhere to go," Felix added, following her.

Maisie and Felix stepped into the family quarters with its plain furniture and paneled walls.

She touched that shard of porcelain again. Usually, she and Felix didn't keep secrets from each other. But what if she showed it to him and he made her march right back to the Woman in Pink and give it to her? What if he lectured her on right and wrong the way he sometimes did? No, Maisie decided. She would keep it to herself. For now.

In New York, Maisie and Felix had slept in the same room divided by a scrim that their mother had kept from her actress days—*a struggling actress,* she always said now that she'd put acting behind her. A *scrim* was a drop curtain that looked opaque in some lights and transparent in others. They had fun playing with the lamps in their bedroom, rearranging them and turning them on and off for effect. But here they each had proper bedrooms that were blandly identical.

Felix lay in bed trying to read, but the noises the house made were too distracting. It creaked. It sighed. It moaned. All he could think of were the things the Woman in Pink had hinted at: ghosts, and worse.

"You awake?" Maisie called from across the hall.

"Yes," Felix said. He put down his book and put on his glasses.

"Can I come in?" Maisie said.

She didn't wait for an answer. She just walked in with her curly hair all tangled and her face with crease marks from the waffle pattern on her blanket. The rain had cooled things down, and Maisie wore her favorite Mets polar fleece vest and flannel pajama bottoms. Felix shivered beneath the thin blanket in his faded madras shorts and yellow T-shirt that said CARMINE STREET POOL. He wished he'd bothered to rummage through the warmer clothes still packed in boxes.

Maisie flopped down on the empty bed across from Felix.

"Mom must be having fun, huh?" she asked. "It's almost ten."

Felix shrugged.

After their mother had moved into her office on Thames Street that day, the other lawyers had insisted she go out to dinner with them at Café Zelda's. *You don't mind, do you?* she'd asked them when she'd called. In the background they could hear the sounds of people laughing. *No, no,* they'd insisted, even though they'd wanted her home with them.

"This house," Felix said as Maisie settled into the other twin bed.

"Noisy," Maisie said. She missed the noise on Bethune Street, the traffic, the late night sounds of people leaving nearby restaurants, and even the early morning garbage and delivery trucks. But the noises here were different, all creaky and shuddering.

"Scary," Felix said.

Maisie sighed. "Prison."

"Prison," Felix agreed.

Maisie brightened. "Hey," she said. "Let's break out."

"Huh?"

"Or should I say, break *in*?" Maisie said, laughing.

"Break *in*?" Felix said, afraid he understood exactly what she meant.

"Why not?" Maisie said, excited.

"Because we're not allowed, that's why," Felix said,

hating what a goody-two-shoes he sounded like.

But it was true—his sister liked to break rules, and he liked to follow them. When he listened to her and they got caught, his good intentions did him no good. Like the time their parents had forbidden them from taking home the classroom guinea pig, Jelly Bean, over Christmas break in second grade, and Maisie had convinced him they could hide Jelly Bean in their room and no one would notice. Their mother had noticed all right and had screamed, terrified: *I said no* rodents in this house! *And I meant no* rodents!

"Our relatives built this monstrosity, right? It's technically ours, isn't it?"

"Mom said no," Felix said, knowing it was too late. Maisie was already standing, and her eyes were twinkling. That picture of Great-Aunt Maisie flashed through Felix's mind. His sister would not be happy if he pointed out their resemblance, but he saw it as clear as anything.

"We know the doors are all locked," she said, pacing, her face scrunched up with concentration. "But there must be another way in."

Maisie stopped pacing, a wicked look of glee in her eyes and a satisfied grin on her face. "Or I could lower you down the dumbwaiter, and you could unlock one of the doors for me and let me in."

"No way," Felix said. "You know I'm afraid of heights. Why don't I lower *you* down the dumb dumbwaiter?"

"Because you're smaller than me. You'll fit better." Maisie loved that she was seven minutes older and almost three inches taller than Felix.

"That thing hasn't been used in a million years. What if it doesn't work and I get trapped in there? Or worse?"

"The Gilded Age," Maisie said, imitating the Woman in Pink's trill, "was from 1865 to 1901. So it's only, like, a hundred years old."

"Great," Felix said, following his sister to the kitchen despite his better judgment.

Maisie opened the narrow door and peered inside.

"Looks safe," she said.

Felix tried to decide what he was more frightened of: getting into the thing, traveling down three flights in it, or running through the big, empty mansion at night to let his sister in.

"Maisie?" he said, taking one tentative step inside. "Do you think kids did this a hundred years ago?"

"Definitely," she said. "I bet Great-Aunt Maisie did it!"

She gave him a shove, and he stumbled all the

way in. The air was stale, reminding Felix of the smell in their apartment in New York after his father smoked one of his forbidden cigars. That comforted him a little, but he still didn't move his foot enough to let Maisie close the door. Felix looked around. The walls were the yellow of fancy mustard, with long cracks here and there and lots of peeling paint. The floor had black-and-gray squares with scuff marks on them.

"Bon voyage," Maisie said cheerfully, catching him off guard and pushing the door shut.

"Hey!" Felix said, pulling his foot in fast, but she was already pressing the button and sending the dumbwaiter—and Felix—downward. The dumbwaiter groaned, then began its slow descent.

He was relieved it was not too tight in there. Plenty of room for a cart of food, he supposed. Felix tried to imagine the fancy breakfasts that had ridden in the thing. Maybe croissants and pain au chocolat like their father used to bring home on Saturday mornings. The now-familiar ache for the past filled him, and Felix wrapped his arms around himself.

Slightly short of breath, he tried to pretend he was somewhere more interesting than a narrow dumbwaiter in an old mansion. But it didn't help. He was right here, and it was dark and airless and scary.

"Maisie?" he called.

To his surprise, her voice came to him as clear as anything. "We're going straight to that room with all the stuff in it."

"The Treasure Chest?" he yelled back to her.

This time she didn't answer. Despite how stuffy it was in the dumbwaiter, goose bumps traveled up Felix's arms. Would this thing ever reach the bottom?

Right then, the dumbwaiter stopped with a small *thud*. Felix opened his eyes. Out the small window on the door he saw nothing but the shaft. He hadn't landed. He was stuck somewhere in the middle. He remembered how his parents forbade them from playing in elevators with their friends who lived in high-rises. *Elevators look innocent enough,* his mother had told him, *but do you know how many kids get hurt goofing around in them?* Now here he was in something even creakier than an elevator. At least elevators had those inspection stickers in them. He was certain no one had inspected this thing lately. Possibly ever.

"Maisie?" he called again.

She still didn't answer. He didn't like being in here, and he didn't like his sister taking off before he even reached the bottom. How would she know which door he opened for her if she'd gone somewhere? Felix shivered. What if he was stuck in here for hours?

Suddenly the dumbwaiter jerked sharply, paused, then hiccupped back to life.

Felix didn't realize he had been holding his breath until he started moving again. If he made it out of here, he was going to tell his sister that he would never listen to her stupid ideas again.

Finally the dumbwaiter landed, more gently than Felix had expected. He pushed the door open with trembling, sweaty hands.

When he peered out, it took a moment for his eyes to adjust to the dark. He blinked and stared out. He was in the large Kitchen with the wooden cabinets filled with fancy china and deep sinks and copper pots and pans. The Woman in Pink had told them that the walls were covered with white subway tiles like the ones in the 14th Street subway station near their old apartment. That had sent a shot of nostalgia through Felix then. Now they gleamed eerily in the one dim light that was turned on.

Felix stepped out carefully, trying to remember the layout of the house. The Kitchen was technically in the Basement, and he had to figure out how to get upstairs to The Treasure Chest. *The Treasure Chest.* Even thinking of it made him shudder. He remembered how nervous the Woman in Pink got when they looked inside that room. In his opinion, anything hidden behind a secret stairway had a good reason to stay hidden. Maybe he could convince Maisie to explore a different room. Like the Ballroom, with its panels imported from France—or was it Italy? Felix couldn't keep all the boring facts straight—and its chandelier made of Venetian glass—or was it Waterford crystal? The Woman in Pink had thrown around both of those things like they actually meant something to two twelve-year-olds.

Or they could slide down the banister of the Grand Staircase, the way their mother had told them Great-Aunt Maisie had done. He thought again of that picture of her as a little girl. No matter how hard he tried, he couldn't believe that the old woman he knew had ever been that girl. *What would she do if she were here right now?* he wondered. If that other Great-Aunt Maisie, the young one, could take his hand and slide down the banister with him? Or run from bedroom to bedroom and jump on all the beds? *That would be fun,* Felix thought, imagining the clouds of dust that would fly out of those untouched bedspreads. If he could meet that little girl, that long ago Maisie, he might feel differently about the poor old one stuck in that assisted living place. Wouldn't it be something if The Treasure Chest could do something like that?

From behind him, the dumbwaiter interrupted his thoughts by making a strange and frightening noise like it was moving. Felix held his breath. Why had he listened to Maisie? He knew better. Yes, there was definitely something in there, and it was definitely moving. Felix tried to run, but he felt like one of those marble statues that dotted the lawn.

The door of the dumbwaiter flew open, and Felix screamed a loud and strangled scream.

· CHAPTER FIVE ·

The Letter

"It's just me," Maisie said, unfolding herself and climbing out of the dumbwaiter. "I called it back up and jumped in."

Felix still couldn't find his voice, even as he watched his sister walk toward him, shaking her head in disgust.

"I got bored waiting up there," she said.

Apparently, she wasn't bored anymore. Her eyes shone in a way that Felix knew meant trouble.

"Want to go and slide down the banister?" he finally managed to say. He imitated sliding with his hand, swooshing it through the air.

Maisie laughed. "No way. We're going straight to The Treasure Chest. Something exciting goes on in there, and we're going to find out what it is."

Felix thought of that hidden stairway and the red velvet ropes that hung in the room's doorway. Ropes were meant to keep people out.

"Maybe we couldn't go in because it's dangerous," Felix said, racing to catch up to his sister who was already heading for the Kitchen stairs.

"Loose floorboards!" he called to her back. "Crumbling ceilings! That kind of thing."

Of course, she ignored him and ran up the stairs that led to the Dining Room.

Felix had no choice. He ran up them, too. But when he reached the Dining Room, Maisie had already disappeared. The table set with its fancy china and silver looked creepy in the darkness. Quickly, Felix scurried out of there and into the Grand Ballroom, which was even creepier still. Earlier today, the marble had been all shiny and pretty, and the giant chandelier had sparkled. But now, as he walked across the floor, his footsteps echoed eerily, and the room had a distinct chill that made him think of ghosts.

"Hello?" Felix called. His voice echoed in the high-ceilinged, empty hallway. "Maisie?"

Felix took tentative steps toward the Grand Staircase.

"Maisie?"

There was silence. And then her voice, far off and small. "Come on, slowpoke! I'm almost there."

Felix walked cautiously through the dark, passing room after room. The Ladies' Drawing Room, the Cigar Room, the Gentlemen's Waiting Room—each distorted and shadowy in the moonlight. His knees were trembling so much that they knocked into each other as he climbed the Grand Staircase. He paused at Great-Aunt Maisie's picture hanging there and, in that instant, Felix could have sworn her eyes actually twinkled. He could have sworn the girl in the picture actually *smiled* at him. A shiver ran straight up his arms.

He blinked. Twice. No, he decided, the picture was just a picture. Relieved, he practically ran the rest of the way up the stairs. At the top, in the hallway, the wall gaped open, revealing the secret stairway that led up to The Treasure Chest. What if his sister had gone up there and something terrible had happened to her? He tried to remember what the Woman in Pink had told them. Strange noises? Transparent women floating around?

"Are you okay?" Felix called from the bottom of the stairs.

When she didn't answer him, he took a deep breath and slowly climbed the narrow stairway.

Maisie had unclipped the red velvet rope, and
Felix saw her standing inside The Treasure Chest,
her face full of wonder.

"Look at all this stuff," she said.

Felix took another deep breath and stepped over
the threshold, half expecting an alarm to go off.

But instead the room was hushed as if it were
holding its breath. The walls were a blue that
made Felix think of the ocean, and the lighter
blue ceiling had puffy white clouds painted
on it. That combination gave him the feeling
that he was at sea or floating. Despite only a bit
of moonlight coming in through the Tiffany
glass window, The Treasure Chest seemed to
be bathed in a soft amber light. Felix glanced
around but couldn't find the source of the light.
A massive desk, smack in the middle, dominated.
Bookshelves lined each wall. In one corner stood
a large globe on a pedestal. There were tables here
and there, but every surface of them and the desk
was covered with stuff: clocks, stones, small boxes,
feathers, papers, buttons, hats, seashells, animal
pelts, rings, china cups, quill pens, a compass,
paper of all kinds—parchment, papyrus, lined
notebook, typing, wallpaper, sandpaper—chunks
of jade and amethyst.

"She said he was a collector," Felix said.

"But why would he want something like this?"
Maisie said, picking up a feather.

"Maybe we shouldn't touch anything," Felix said.
To his relief, she put it down.

But then she picked up something else, a faded
scroll from the desk. Carefully, she unrolled it.
The paper was old and stiff and about twice the size
of a sheet of computer paper.

"What is it?" Felix said.

"A list of some kind," Maisie said, frowning.

"Like a shopping list?"

When Maisie didn't answer him, Felix decided
to look for himself. He reached over and tried to
snatch the paper from his sister's hand before she
could resist. But when he grabbed onto it, Maisie
yanked it back. Their eyes met across the desk,
their hands clutching the paper.

The room filled with the deafening sounds
of gunfire. The air smelled of sulfur and smoke.
Felix tried to let go of the paper, but he couldn't.
It was as if his hand was superglued to it. They were
each aware of being lifted ever so slightly off the
ground. Maisie's toes barely reached the carpet.

From outside the stained-glass window came the
sound of their mother's car on the long driveway,
Great-Aunt Maisie's old blue 1967 Mustang that was
in desperate need of a new muffler.

Startled, Maisie let go of the paper. As soon as she did, the air smelled like it usually did, all musty and mothbally. She and Felix were both jolted back down onto the carpet.

"Were we just . . . um . . . in the air?" Felix said.

"Sort of." Maisie gulped.

"Like . . . about to fly or something?" Felix asked. His heart beat so hard and so loud that he thought he might be having a heart attack. People *could* actually get scared to death, couldn't they?

"I don't know," Maisie said. Her eyes darted around the room as if she might find an explanation. Her heart was beating hard and loud, too, but she wasn't afraid. Instead, Maisie was more excited than she'd ever been in her whole life.

"We started to *fly*!" she said, the idea slowly sinking in.

"Maisie," Felix said evenly, "that is not a good thing."

"You're right," Maisie said. "It's a great thing. An amazing thing."

Felix studied the paper he was still holding. "It's a list of names," he said.

"Thousands of them."

Maisie peered over his shoulder at the fancy, old-fashioned writing. One brief paragraph at the start and then all of those names. Despite the dimness of the room, Maisie could just make out some of the names: Benjamin Thacher. Henry Morse. James Ellis . . . they seemed to be in categories of some kind.

"Oh! I get it!" she said. "They're arranged by states," Maisie said, pointing. "See?"

Massachusetts. New York. Connecticut . . .

The Mustang's car door slammed shut, and the sound of their mother's footsteps on the circular drive echoed in the still night.

Felix dropped the paper back onto the desk. "Let's get out of here," he said.

But Maisie picked the scroll up again and started to read the names to herself, her lips moving slightly as she did. *John Dunlop . . . Jacob Hart . . .*

"Put it down!" Felix said. "We have only a few minutes to get into our beds and pretend to be asleep!"

He was halfway down the stairs before he realized that his sister had not followed him. Felix ran back to find Maisie still standing exactly in the same spot, still reading the list of names.

"Put it down!" Felix yelled again. "Mom'll be in the house any second."

He could practically hear their mother struggling with the key. Luckily for them, the key was tricky and had to be put in the lock just so, with the door held just right, for it to work.

That would slow her down at least.

"Come on!" he said.

Carefully, Maisie began to roll the paper and tuck it under her arm.

"You can't take it with you," Felix said.

"Why not? No one's going to notice it's missing."

"Look," he said, starting to panic, "something happened to us just now. Something weird. What if it has to do with that piece of paper? You really want to take it into your room?"

Maisie hesitated. "I don't think it's the paper. I think it's something in this room. That's why we're supposed to stay out." This was the most exciting thing that had ever happened to her, and she just had to figure out what it meant. And how to do it again.

"But we're not allowed in lots of rooms," Felix reminded her, afraid of what she might be thinking.

"That's because there's something disintegrating inside. Like fragile rugs or rickety furniture. Everything in here is pretty solid. Something else makes them keep everyone out."

"We can come back tomorrow when Mom goes to work," Felix said desperately. "But if we get caught in here now, we'll never get to the bottom of it. They'll probably padlock everything shut."

Maisie sighed. "Fine," she said. She hated how logical Felix could be. "I just hope Mom doesn't see us pop out of the dumbwaiter."

"There's no time for that. We have to get over to the servants' stairs. Fast."

Felix ran out, but Maisie stayed put. Something had caught her eye. She took the shard from her pocket and walked over to the Ming vase standing on its pedestal. Carefully, she fit it into the empty place where her shard belonged. But if her piece was back in its proper place, why was there still a hole in the vase, on the opposite side? Maisie put her finger in that hole. Did Felix also have a shard? Or did someone else?

"Maisie," Felix hissed from the doorway. "Come on!"

"I'm coming, I'm coming," she said. She popped her piece out and slipped it back into her pocket.

They ran out of The Treasure Chest and down the stairs, stopping only to pull the wall back into place before racing down the Grand Staircase and past all of the empty rooms with strange shadows falling across their walls. Maisie reached the door—the one in the Dining Room that led to the back stairs. She tugged as hard as she could, but it didn't budge.

"Locked!" she called over her shoulder.

Felix reached the door, panting.

"We are so dead," he said.

He thought back to their tour with the
Woman in Pink. She'd used a single key to open
the door. He remembered thinking that it was
a little strange that the key wasn't on a ring or
something. So where had that key come from?

"I think the docent keeps the key hidden
here," he said, running his hand along the wall.
He needed a light, a key, a miracle.

"Found it!" Maisie said. "Under the rug, just
like on TV."

She unlocked the door, careful to put the key
back where she'd found it. But when she turned
the handle, the door didn't budge.

"Push!" Felix said. He placed his own bony
shoulder next to his sister's, and the two of them
pushed as hard as they could.

The door flew open, sending them stumbling
onto the staircase landing on the first floor. Just
one flight below, they could hear the sound of
their mother's sensible heels moving closer and,
clear as anything, they recognized the song she
was humming: ABBA's "Mamma Mia."

Maisie and Felix made it into the kitchen
seconds before their mother opened the door and
walked in.

"Mamma mia!" she belted, finishing the song
with a flourish.

Then she saw them standing in front of her. They tried to make their breathing sound even and measured. They tried to appear innocent.

Their mother looked at them, surprised.

"You two are still awake?" she said.

"Scary old house, Mom," Maisie said. "We got frightened."

Felix nodded enthusiastically.

Their mother studied their faces, one at a time, looking from Maisie to Felix and then back again.

"Of course you did," she said finally. "What was I thinking going out tonight? This place can seem pretty creepy."

She opened her arms and pulled the twins in for a hug. Their mother gave great hugs.

"Now bed, please," she said. "It's late."

Felix had to count all the way to forty-nine before his heart finally slowed. But Maisie didn't even try to calm herself. Tomorrow morning, as soon as their mother left for work, they would go back into The Treasure Chest.

In the hallway between their rooms, Maisie and Felix paused.

"I'm never going back in there again," Felix said. "Ever."

Disappointment filled Maisie. "What? Of course you are." Then she added, "*We* are."

Felix shook his head. "No way. You've talked me into crazy things before, but this time I'm not letting you."

"We started to fly!" she said as if he'd forgotten.

"Exactly," Felix said. With that, he walked into his room and firmly closed the door.

Maisie leaned into the door and whispered, "Felix."

"No," he said.

"Just one more time?"

"No," he said again.

She fingered the shard in her pocket. "What if I told you I know something? Something practically magical?"

"Forget it, Maisie. I know that you don't know anything magical. I know you're just trying to get me to open this door and agree to go back into that haunted room."

Maisie sighed, good and loud so Felix would definitely hear her. "Fine then," she said. "I won't show you what I have in my pocket or tell you how that vase is magical or something."

She waited.

The door opened slowly.

"What do you have in your pocket?" Felix asked her suspiciously.

Maisie reached in and took the shard from her

pocket. She opened her hand and held it up for
Felix to see.

"You took part of that expensive vase?" he
asked, his eyes wide. "I can't believe you."

"Remember how the lady said the maintenance
people must have swept up all the pieces?"

Felix nodded.

"Well, the vase in The Treasure Chest is
missing a piece. A piece exactly this size and shape."

Felix considered what she said. "You mean
they glued the thing back together?"

"Oh, please," Maisie said, exasperated. "That
fast? No, you dope. The vase put itself back
together somehow."

"Really?" Felix said. "That's what you think
happened? And you think *I'm* the dope here?"

"I'm telling you. Something magical happened.
That vase in there is the same one that broke."

"Well there's one more reason I'm staying away
from that room. Vases break and get put back
together all by themselves. People fly. And who
knows what else." He turned and began to go back
into his room.

"Wait!" Maisie said. "There's something else."

Despite his better judgment, Felix paused.

"There's another missing piece in the vase,"
Maisie said.

"I guess the magic didn't work so great," Felix said.

"Really? I think someone else has a piece."

They stared at each other.

"One more time," Felix said, taking a big breath. "We'll go back tomorrow morning, and that's it."

Maisie smiled. "One more time," she repeated.

This time she went into her room and closed the door, leaving Felix standing there wondering who had that other piece and how in the world his sister had talked him into doing the very thing he had promised he would not do.

· CHAPTER SIX ·

Great-Aunt Maisie

Maisie woke up late the next morning, ready to get Felix and go directly back into the mansion while their mother went off to her first day at work. Instead she found their mother sitting at the kitchen table wearing her ratty, peach, terry-cloth robe and doing the *New York Times* crossword puzzle.

"What are you doing home?" Maisie said, surprised.

"Nice to see you, too," her mother said. She narrowed her eyes at Maisie. "Are you two up to something?"

"Yeah. We're watching *Escape from Alcatraz* to get some ideas."

"Funny, Maisie," her mother said, sighing.

She held up a mixing bowl. "Crepes?" she said.

"Sure," Maisie mumbled.

Her mother went to the stove and began preparing the batter and the pan.

"So, do you have the *whole* day off?" Maisie asked.

"I've got to take care of a few things for Great-Aunt Maisie," she said. "Once I start working, it's going to be hard to run all of her errands for her. They let me get my office organized yesterday and deal with Great-Aunt Maisie today. That way I can hit the ground running on Wednesday as a lawyer at Fishbaum and Fishbaum! I was hoping to start on Thursday when you two start school, but I didn't want to push my luck."

Maisie sighed. How could she wait twenty-four whole hours to go back in The Treasure Chest? She had hardly slept at all last night, her mind racing with possibilities. Would they actually be able to fly? And if they did, would they be able to fly out of Elm Medona, maybe all the way back to Bethune Street? Thinking about it now made Maisie tingle with anticipation.

Until her mother said, "I thought we'd go visit Great-Aunt Maisie after breakfast."

"Great," Maisie said flatly.

"Now, now. Without her, I don't know what we would have done."

"Stayed in New York, maybe? Where we belong?"

Maisie said. There was almost nothing worse than visiting Great-Aunt Maisie in the nursing home.

"Stop dwelling on the past," her mother said.

Thankfully, Felix came into the kitchen before their mother started her lecture about how lucky they all were to be there.

When he saw their mother at the stove mixing batter, Felix felt relieved. He hadn't slept well last night, worrying over all the terrifying things that might happen when they went back in The Treasure Chest. Hadn't he smelled gunpowder in there? Hadn't he heard gunshots? And when he remembered the feeling of his toes scraping the floor, then lifting just enough to have no floor at all beneath him, he shuddered.

"She's got the *whole* day off," Maisie said to him. "They're letting her start *tomorrow.*"

"Really? That's great," Felix said, unable to hide his enthusiasm.

Their mother kissed him on the top of his head. "I'm glad someone around here thinks so," she said.

He dipped a finger in the batter for a taste and managed to get some before she swatted him away.

"Mmmm," he said, licking his finger. "Crepes."

"Nutella?" their mother asked. "Or lemon?"

"Nutella," Maisie said, flopping onto one of the chairs at the table.

"Lemon," Felix said, sitting at the other end.

Their eyes met across the red, enamel tabletop, and he shrugged.

"Tomorrow's another day," he said.

A few moments later, their mother slid crepes in front of Felix and Maisie.

Maisie glared at her brother. "Tomorrow it is," she said.

The nursing home where Great-Aunt Maisie lived was called Island Retirement Center. It had a view of the bay from the big dining room and the family room, but the bedrooms where the residents spent most of their time were small and square and looked out on the parking lot. Great-Aunt Maisie's room was painted a cheerful yellow color, and she had a vase full of peonies—her favorite flower—but the room still felt depressing. The smell of cafeteria food and rubbing alcohol lingered everywhere, and the sight of all those old people sitting in wheelchairs made Felix and Maisie sad.

Today, with the low gray clouds and haze, the place looked even worse. To distract herself from how grim it was in there, Maisie counted how many people passed them using walkers, how many sat in the hall in their wheelchairs, and how many walked by on their own. The wheelchairs won. By a lot.

In fact, Great-Aunt Maisie was sitting in a wheelchair, dressed in a red Chanel suit with the Chanel Red lipstick she always insisted the nurse put on her. Maisie hated the way the lipstick bled into the lines around her great-aunt's mouth and that she got all dressed up like that just to sit in her room all day.

In first grade, they had to make dolls with dried-apple faces. They used yarn for the dolls' hair and got to fashion clothes for them out of scraps of fabric and ribbon, but those withered apple faces still looked sad no matter how cheerfully they were dressed. Great-Aunt Maisie kind of reminded Maisie of those apple dolls, which made her feel bad for her.

When she told Felix that, he said she was being mean. "She's old, and she had a stroke," Felix said. "She can't help it." That was the other thing that made Maisie squirm: Half of Great-Aunt Maisie's face pulled way to the left from the stroke, and when she tried to talk, it came out all garbled.

"Be nice," her mother whispered to Maisie as they walked over to Great-Aunt Maisie's good side.

Felix kissed the old woman on her good cheek,

but Maisie hung back.

"How's the house treating you?" Great-Aunt Maisie asked, except, of course, it didn't exactly sound like that.

"The house is fine," their mother said loudly, enunciating each word.

Felix started to move away, but Great-Aunt Maisie grabbed his arm.

"How do you like the house?" she asked him, her blue eyes penetrating his.

Something about the way she looked at him made Felix think she knew what they had done. He glanced over at Maisie, but she was pretending to look at the orchids so she didn't have to look at Great-Aunt Maisie.

"It's great," Felix said.

"Have you been downstairs?"

"Downstairs?" he asked. How could she know?

"They had a lovely tour," their mother said.

"Have you been downstairs?" Great-Aunt Maisie asked him again, her eyes never wavering.

"Uh. Yeah," Felix said. He wished Maisie would pay attention, help him out here. She was a good liar when she needed to be.

Great-Aunt Maisie smiled crookedly. "Yes?" she said.

"They had a very good tour," their mother

said again, louder this time, even though Great-Aunt Maisie wasn't at all deaf. "Why don't we go to the dining room and have some lunch?"

"Good idea," Maisie said, relieved to get out of the room. She would eat a grilled cheese sandwich and one of those little ice creams that came in a plastic container with its own wooden spoon and be home in no time.

But Great-Aunt Maisie still held on to Felix's arm. "Elm Medona," she said, and it was the clearest thing he'd heard her say since she had the stroke. She nodded at him. "Elm Medona."

"I'm afraid poor Great-Aunt Maisie is declining," their mother said in the car after lunch. "She couldn't understand anything today."

Felix disagreed. He thought she was trying to tell him something. But what? Elm Medona. He wrote it with his finger on the leg of his jeans. Why had she repeated it like that? And how had she figured out that they'd gone into the house on their own? She'd grown up there, so it made sense that she knew about whatever happened in The Treasure Chest.

"Earth to Felix," Maisie was saying. "Now Mom wants to take us shopping for school stuff."

Felix groaned.

"Poor Great-Aunt Maisie," their mother said again, pointing the car toward Warwick and the shopping mall there. "Well, at least she had a very interesting life."

Felix caught Maisie's eye, but she had no idea that Great-Aunt Maisie had been trying to tell him something. *Elm Medona,* he thought. He'd always assumed it was just a particular type of elm tree.

"What does it mean?" he asked his mother. "Elm Medona?"

His mother shrugged. "I have no idea."

Maisie looked up, interested. "Why do you want to know all of a sudden?" she asked suspiciously.

Felix looked out the car window. "Just curious," he said.

+ + + + +

The next morning, as soon as their mother left for work, Maisie walked into Felix's room.

"Come on, get up," she said. "We're alone at last."

"I've been thinking about it," he said, already sitting up with a yellow legal pad on his knees. "We have to wait until tonight."

"Give me a break," Maisie said. "Your delay tactics are not going to work. I've been waiting forever already."

Felix shook his head. "No, I promised I'd go back one more time, and I will. But we have to do everything exactly the same, or nothing will happen."

"All we need to do is go in there before the first tour starts, and—"

"And?" Felix asked.

"I don't know. But I can't wait to find out."

Felix handed her the pad. "I wrote down everything we did that night so that we can do it the same way."

Maisie barely looked at what he'd written. "The first tour is at ten. That gives us almost an hour."

"I'm telling you, we have to do it at night." He pointed to number two on his list.

"Have I ever misled you?" Maisie said. She pointed her finger at him. "Don't answer that."

He knew his sister well enough to know that she wouldn't believe him until her plan failed. So he followed her out of the apartment and down the stairs.

"Here's my surprise," she told him as they stood in front of the door on the first landing. "I didn't lock the door when we left the other night. So we can walk right down the stairs."

"Number three," Felix said. "The dumbwaiter."

"Oh, please."

Maisie opened the door. "Ta-da!" she said, and then bounded into the Dining Room.

"This is *so* not going to work," Felix muttered. The sound of a vacuum cleaner made him stop walking. "Listen," he said.

Maisie paused. "It's just the cleaners. There was a big fund-raiser here last night."

She made her way through the Dining Room, still set for dinner, and into the Grand Ballroom. Tiptoeing across the marble floor, she didn't bother to glance at the fancy rooms she passed as she approached the Grand Staircase. But Felix did. He glimpsed the gold trim and ornate moldings in the Ladies' Drawing Room, the medieval tapestries and imported fireplaces in the Cigar Room, the chandelier made in Belgium hanging in Ariane Pickworth's study. He couldn't explain it, but it was as if everything in the house was watching them.

Maisie sprinted up the Grand Staircase, but Felix stopped along the way to stare at the photograph of Great-Aunt Maisie with Great-Uncle Thorne at its edge. *What did they know?* he wondered, and as he thought it, a shiver crept up his arms.

Slowly, he climbed the rest of the stairs, feeling with each step he took that the very house was alive.

In the hallway, Maisie waited for him, pacing. Just like the Woman in Pink had done, she touched the fancy wall, and it opened noiselessly, revealing the hidden staircase. *Would the magic of seeing that staircase appear like that ever fade?* Felix thought as he gasped again.

When she reached The Treasure Chest, Maisie unhooked the rope and held it up for Felix to enter.

"No, no," he said. "You should go in first, do exactly what you did the other night, and then I'll come in."

"Time is passing here, bro," Maisie said impatiently.

"Fine," he said, and walked in.

Maisie went right to the desk and picked up the scroll. She closed her eyes and waited.

Felix stared at her. "We did something to make it start up," he said. "Or we did lots of things."

She opened her eyes. "All I remember is that it smelled like fireworks, there were loud popping sounds, and then the next thing I knew, I was lifted off the floor." She held the scroll out to him. "Here. You hold it."

Felix pulled it away from her.

Nothing.

"Actually," he said, "it was unrolled."

Carefully, he unrolled the paper, revealing the list of names in neat rows, written in ink that had long since faded, the letters all curlicues and loops and swirls.

He closed his eyes. The vacuum cleaner grew louder.

"Nothing," he said. "It's not the paper. It's . . . I don't know, maybe it's something we said. Like an incantation."

Maisie stamped her foot. "Come on, ghost or whatever you are," she said.

"I think the cleaners are getting closer," Felix said. "We better get out of here."

"Phinneas Pickworth, are you listening?" she said.

Nothing.

Maybe Felix was right. Maybe they had to recreate that night exactly. The sound of the vacuum grew louder. Maisie sighed.

"Okay," she said reluctantly. "Where's your list?"

Even though she thought it was ridiculous, Maisie did everything Felix told her to later that night after Mom went to sleep. She put on the exact clothes she'd worn that night—her flannel pajama bottoms and Mets fleece vest—even though the cold snap they'd had that night was gone and the heat had come back. Felix found his faded madras shorts under his bed and the yellow T-shirt thrown over a chair. After Felix went down in the dumbwaiter, Maisie waited the exact amount of time she'd waited the other night, then she got in the dumbwaiter herself.

As the dumbwaiter made its way down slowly, Maisie's stomach flitted with excitement. When she was younger, she always threw up before her birthday party or right when she had to give a class presentation. "You're ruled by your gut," her father liked to say. Thinking of him made her sad. She tried to picture him in Doha, a city she'd only seen on Google Earth, with its crescent-shaped bay and tall skyscrapers. But she couldn't imagine him so far away in such an exotic place. To Maisie, he was always walking across Bleecker Street toward home.

The dumbwaiter reached the bottom, and Maisie climbed out.

"You lead the way," Felix said softly. "Like last time."

By the slump of his sister's shoulders, he could tell she was feeling sad.

"I miss him, too," Felix called after her.

She turned around. "I know," she said.

She started to walk again but stopped. "Sometimes I pretend he's just out for the day, you know. That any minute he'll walk in the door . . ."

Felix, choked up at the idea of seeing their father like that, could only nod.

Maisie squeezed her brother's hand. "Maybe that's it. Maybe you go in that room and make a wish, and it comes true."

"That would be nice," Felix said, even though he knew better.

This time, he followed her across the marble floor of the Grand Ballroom and up the Grand Staircase, letting Maisie have the lead like she had that first time. He paused at that photograph of Great-Aunt Maisie as a little girl. Then he called Maisie's name, just like he did that night, and she called back, "In here."

Felix climbed the hidden stairway, and when he got to The Treasure Chest, Maisie had the list in her hand. So far, they had recreated everything perfectly.

He walked into the room. "What is that?" he asked, pleased that he'd written out a script and made them each memorize it. He couldn't remember exactly how everything had happened that night, but he thought he was pretty close.

"A list of some kind," Maisie said.

"Like a shopping list?"

She didn't answer him, and he smiled. *Perfect*, he thought.

Maisie handed him the list. Her stomach was churning so much that she thought she really might throw up.

Felix took the list and held his breath.

Nothing.

They waited for a long time.

"What are we forgetting?" Felix finally said.

Maisie tried to remember. She'd had the list in her hands, and she was reading it, wondering who all the people on it were. And Felix asked her if it was a shopping list. They'd talked about the fact that the names were arranged by state, too. Or was that after they heard their mother drive up?

"I don't know," she said.

"Maybe it was something special about that night," Felix said. "Like maybe it was a full moon or an eclipse or something like that."

Maisie sighed. That sounded like a real possibility. Full moons made all sorts of things happen.

"That means we'd have to wait a whole month before we can come back," she said.

"Or longer if it's a lunar eclipse or planets lining up a certain way," Felix added, trying not to sound relieved.

Maisie looked so upset that he added, "But it's probably the moon. I mean, that even affects tides and stuff, right?"

"We finally have something to look forward to again," Maisie said, trying not to cry, "and it gets snatched away, just like everything else."

"No, Maisie," Felix said, putting his arm

around her, "we'll figure it out. I mean, you will, anyway. You're like a genius in science and stuff." He didn't know what he would do if his sister actually started to cry. Maisie never cried.

"It's so unfair!" she said, squirming away from him. Her eyes flared with anger now. "Why did our stupid parents have to get divorced? Why did we have to move to stupid Rhode Island? Why did we get stuck living in servants' quarters?"

Her anger actually made Felix feel better. This was the Maisie he was used to.

"And now we can't even fly or whatever it was we almost did!"

Felix burst out laughing. "Yeah," he said. "We can't even fly."

She glared at him. "Oh! Shut up!" she yelled, which made him laugh even harder.

Maisie moved toward the door. "You wait," she said, spinning around and pointing at him. "I'm going to figure this out, and I might not even take you with me next time."

Before he could protest, she was out the door and down the stairs.

"And if you don't come right now, I'm closing you in there for the night!" she yelled.

Felix ran out of there as fast as he could. She was just mad enough to actually do it.

· CHAPTER SEVEN ·

Landing

"I didn't give you the paper!" Maisie whispered, shaking Felix hard. "You tried to grab it from me."

"What are you talking about?" he muttered, rolling away from her.

"Wake up!" she said. "We have to go back and do it all over again. Except this time you have to grab the paper from me."

Felix managed to get one eye open. The clock on his nightstand glowed 2:08. He groaned.

"Remember? I didn't want you to have it. I was reading the names, and you grabbed it from me."

"That's right," Felix said, remembering.

"Come on," Maisie ordered. "Get up."

He knew he didn't have a choice. He climbed out

of bed and followed his sister into the dark hallway.

Maisie paused at their mother's bedroom door. Ever since the divorce, she slept with the television on, and Maisie could hear Jerry Seinfeld's voice and then canned laughter coming from in there. But nothing else. On tiptoes, she kept going. In the kitchen, their dinner plates still sat on the table, the orange sauce from their mac and cheese all hard and crusty now. Another thing that started after the divorce. Their parents used to always clean up after dinner, singing show tunes together as they washed and dried and swept. *They had seemed like two people in love,* she thought.

With a sigh, she opened the door to the dumbwaiter and watched as Felix climbed inside for the second time that night.

"Bon voyage," she said as she closed it.

But Felix stopped her from closing the door the whole way.

"No matter what happens in there," he said, "we're not doing this again, right?"

"Right," Maisie said.

"I want you to promise me," Felix said.

"Okay, okay. I promise."

"No matter what happens," he insisted. "Even if we somehow land in Dad's living room or . . . or . . . I don't know, back on Bethune Street."

"I said I promise."

He studied his sister's determined face.

"I mean," he said carefully, "what if we woke up or whatever, and we were in our old bedroom and Mom and Dad were in the kitchen singing—"

"Is that what you think?" Maisie said. "We're going to go back in time?"

"No," Felix said carefully. "I don't know what to think."

Maisie closed the door, pressed the white button, and watched her brother disappear.

In the quiet, dark kitchen that smelled faintly of mac and cheese, Maisie pressed her forehead against the door of the dumbwaiter. Somehow, getting back into The Treasure Chest and maybe flying again—flying off somewhere, even!—had become the most important thing in the world to her. Ever since her parents had sat them down at that diner back in New York and told them they were getting divorced, nothing seemed to matter to Maisie. Even standing here right now, she could still remember how the French fry in her mouth grew cold and how her stomach jumped at the news. *I think I'm going to throw up*, she had said, pushing her way out of the booth where she sat knee to knee with Felix. She hadn't made it to the bathroom, throwing up instead right in the middle of the restaurant.

Soon afterward, the diner closed down, her father moved to Qatar, and she and Felix were in a U-Haul heading north with their mother. Until they stood together in The Treasure Chest with the smell of sulfur and all the noisy banging and popping, getting literally swept off their feet, Maisie had wondered if she would ever care about anything again. Now she did. The Treasure Chest, she believed, would change everything.

The dumbwaiter made its noisy landing below her, and Maisie called it back up. When it arrived, she closed the door fast, managing to press the button again to send herself downward just in time. As she inched down, she closed her eyes and whispered, "Please work this time, please work this time, please work this time," until she, too, landed in the dark, cavernous kitchen.

Once again Maisie emerged, and Felix pretended to be startled. True, she had thought his insistence on exactly reenacting what they'd done that first time was a bit extreme. In fact, Felix's imagination always seemed a bit extreme to Maisie. But maybe this time he was right. It was worth trying it his way. She had to. She was desperate.

✚ ✚ ✚ ✚ ✚

Maisie did everything perfectly. As she waited for Felix to catch up to her in The Treasure Chest, she unrolled the scroll and glanced at all those names. She couldn't help wondering what had happened to all of the men. The paragraph on the top left corner looked like a letter of some kind. But before she could read it, Felix arrived. Maisie's stomach rolled nervously.

"What is that?" he asked.

"A list of some kind," Maisie said.

"Like a shopping list?"

He grabbed it, tugging it from her hands.

And then, it started.

"Maisie?" she heard Felix say, but his voice sounded small and funny.

That smell of gunpowder filled the room, and then they felt themselves being lifted. But this time, nothing stopped them from rising higher and higher and actually being carried away, almost the way it feels in the brief moment before a roller coaster drops you from its highest hill. A warm wind whipped around them. It smelled of everything good: cinnamon and Christmas trees and salty ocean air; fresh lemons and hot chocolate and a flower garden. It smelled like home.

They held their breaths.

Maisie cracked her eyes open enough to see the startled look on her brother's face. He had his eyes opened wide, and his mouth was formed into an

O. His hair stood straight up in the wind, and his arms waved about, trying to find balance.

She somersaulted, the taste of mac and cheese rising in her throat. Then they dropped. For a nanosecond there was nothing. No smells. No sounds. No motion.

Then they landed. Hard.

Maisie blinked and looked around. She was in the middle of a barn. It was daylight. She smelled animals and hay and earth. A cow mooed.

"Felix?"

"I think I broke my arm," Felix said. He was lying across the barn floor from her.

Outside, she saw green pastures, leafy trees, and off in the distance, rooftops. She walked to her brother, the paper still in her hand.

A shadow fell across them. A girl wearing a bonnet, a long, brown dress, and a white apron stood frowning at them.

"Pardon me?" she said softly.

Felix and Maisie glanced at each other, then up at the girl. She looked to be about their age, small and serious.

She cleared her throat and stepped closer to them.

"Well," the girl said, "what have we here?"

"Um," Felix said. But he could not think of anything else to say. He rubbed the sore place on his arm and winced.

The girl waited.

Maisie peered at her. Except for the old-fashioned clothing, she looked completely ordinary. She did not look like she belonged in Doha, Maisie decided. So whatever had happened to them did not bring them where she most wanted to go. Second most, she wanted to be back in New York City. A cow mooed again. She definitely wasn't in New York City, either.

"Where are we?" Maisie asked. She wondered if the shard she'd tucked in her pocket was still there. She reached inside the pocket of her fleece, and her fingers touched the smooth, hard porcelain. Finding it there comforted her, even though this girl was awkwardly staring at her.

"All of this land belongs to Captain Stephen Barton," the girl said with the slightest hint of a lisp. "My father."

The name meant absolutely nothing to Maisie. When she met Felix's eyes, he shrugged.

Maisie swallowed hard. "I'm Maisie Robbins," she said. "And this is my brother, Felix."

The girl studied them carefully. Then she held out her hand.

"Clara Barton," she said. "Pleased to meet you. Now can you tell me what you're doing in my barn?"

·CHAPTER EIGHT·

Clara Barton

Maisie watched the girl intently. She had dark hair topped with a bonnet of some kind, and she wore a long, loose dress and black granny boots that laced up the front. As Maisie looked around the barn, a slow realization came to her. She knew exactly where they had landed. Filled with disappointment, she kneeled beside Felix, who lay sprawled and dazed on the ground.

"Come on," she said. "Get up. Mom is going to kill us for sure."

If their mother hadn't been so adamant about them not having cell phones, Maisie would have called her right there and then. She almost laughed, imagining her mother's surprise when she heard where they were.

Clara kneeled, too. She gently prodded Felix's arm. Clara shook her head. "I do not think it's broken," she said.

Maisie looked at her, surprised. "Well, I think we need an X-ray to be sure. If we can use your phone and call our mother—" Maisie stopped.

The girl was staring at her in complete confusion.

"Oh. Right. You're not allowed to have telephones," Maisie said.

Clara continued to stare at Maisie.

"Haven't you ever seen anyone in her pajamas before?" Maisie said.

Clara didn't answer. She just kept staring. Finally, she pointed to the logo on Maisie's fleece jacket. "Are you in a society of some kind?" she asked.

"What? This?" Maisie said, fingering the blue-and-orange stitching that said NY METS. She laughed. "Well, sure. Of course you don't know about baseball. You don't have TV or even a radio, right?"

Felix looked even more puzzled than the girl. His face was pale, and his arm hurt. Badly. He didn't care what this kid thought. Felix was certain his arm was broken. Below the short, yellow sleeve of his T-shirt, he saw a red mark right where it hurt most.

"Can we please use your phone?" he asked Clara. He didn't care how mad their mother got, either. If she could come and get them, he would be happy.

Why had he ever let Maisie talk him into this?

"Didn't you hear me? She doesn't have a phone," Maisie said with great authority. "Can't you guess where we are?"

"I don't feel like guessing," Felix muttered.

"No phone. No TV. No radio. No Mets," Maisie said, counting off on her fingers. She leaned close to Felix and whispered, "She's wearing a bonnet."

"I can see that!" he snapped.

"Where are you from?" Clara asked, chewing her bottom lip. "You speak so differently."

"Rhode Island," Felix said.

"Rhode Island and Providence Plantations," Clara said, nodding knowingly.

Maisie and Felix exchanged a glance.

"Is that what you call it?" Maisie said.

Clara blushed. "Isn't that what *you* call it?"

"I think I read that somewhere," Felix said. "Maybe in one of those brochures."

"I love to read!" Clara said. "Dolly taught me. My sister," she added.

"Homeschooling?" Felix groaned.

In their apartment building in New York there was a family who homeschooled their two kids. Every morning, when he and Maisie headed out the door to school, those kids were still in pajamas. They used to rub it in, too. *We spent the day at the*

American Museum of Natural History, they'd say as Maisie and Felix lugged their heavy backpacks down the hall. *We studied the flora and fauna of Central Park.*

Clara was nodding thoughtfully. "Why, yes. I did learn at home. Stephen taught me arithmetic, and Sally taught me geography. But I love to read more than almost anything."

For the first time since they'd landed in the barn, Felix smiled. "So do I," he said.

"I read so much that my parents even sent me off to school," Clara told him. "But I hated being away from home so much, they let me come back," she added softly.

Her shyness touched Felix. Sometimes he felt like that, afraid what he thought or did might seem ridiculous.

"You don't have to go to school?" he asked.

"They're all homeschooled," Maisie said. "I can't believe her parents even let her go away."

"They who?" Felix said.

"The Amish!" Maisie said. "All that trouble and we've landed in Amish country. Just our boring luck."

Three years ago, their parents had rented a car and taken them on a family road trip to Philadelphia and Amish country in Pennsylvania. Maisie had sulked the whole way there because

Marina Martin's family had also gone to
Pennsylvania, but her parents had taken her to
Hershey where the street lamps were shaped like
Kisses, the Hershey factory tour gave out free
chocolate, and the amusement park had something
like five different roller coasters. Maisie and Felix
were stuck staring at the Liberty Bell and watching
people in old-fashioned clothes drive by in horse-
drawn buggies. *This is the worst vacation ever,* she'd said
over and over. Her mother kept reading from a
guidebook and making them do everything it said,
like eating something disgusting called shoofly pie
and looking at hand-sewn quilts.

"Of course," Felix said, his eyes brightening. How
awesome was this? They had gone into The Treasure
Chest and landed in Pennsylvania! "It all adds up.
The bonnet. The dress. Even this barn."

He'd hated that trip, too, though not quite as
much as Maisie. The cheesesteaks in Philly were
good, he'd thought. What he'd hated was how much
their parents had bickered, how their mother
rolled her eyes at almost everything their father
did, and the way their father said, *Fine, Jenny,* like
absolutely nothing at all was fine.

"We're in Bird-in-Hand, Pennsylvania. Again,"
Maisie said.

"You are not in Pennsylvania!" Clara said. She

turned to Felix. "You're in Massachusetts, and you must know that. You must."

Felix glanced over at Maisie.

"There are Amish everywhere," Maisie said, but she didn't sound completely certain. "Not just in Bird-in-Hand, Pennsylvania."

"How would you even get to Pennsylvania?" Clara said, more to herself than to them.

"The point is, we need to get out of Amish country and to the nearest town so we can call Mom," Maisie said.

A new wave of disappointment came over her. Massachusetts? How lame was that? All that planning, all that excitement, and they were only an hour from home.

"At least it's easier to get home from Massachusetts," Felix said.

He stretched his arm and yelped. As if being the new kid wasn't bad enough, he was going to have to start school with his arm in a cast.

"You need to lie down and be still," Clara said. "When my brother David fell, he was fine, too, at first. Three days later the fever came, and he wasn't himself for three more years."

"Three years?" Felix said. He rubbed the spot on his arm that hurt so much.

Clara shook her head. "It was terrible. I was only

eleven that summer. He went to a barn raising, and he was assigned to affix the rafters to the ridge pole—"

"Now who's speaking differently?" Maisie grumbled.

Clara ignored her and kept telling her story. "The timber on which he was standing suddenly collapsed, and he fell to the floor." She shuddered remembering. "But he leaped up immediately. Everyone who saw David get to his feet so quickly was amazed. Mister Goddard called it a 'wondrous escape.' And David claimed he was completely unhurt, except for a headache that plagued him all of that day."

Felix put his hand to his head and pressed. No headache. Just the throbbing in his arm right above the elbow.

"Then the fever came," Clara said softly. "When it continued after seven days, when fevers usually stop—"

Maisie, clearly bored, had started to pace.

"Do you know what Doctor Finigan has our mother do when we get fevers?" Felix asked Clara. "Doctor Finigan has her alternate Tylenol and Motrin. The kid stuff, you know? It almost always works."

Clara patted her apron pockets. "I wish I had something to write with so I could make a note of that." She blushed. "I very much want to become a nurse. To help others who need it."

"A nurse?" Maisie laughed. "And change bedpans all day? If you're so smart, you should go to med school and be a doctor."

"A doctor?" Clara said, and she laughed, too. "In case you haven't noticed, I'm a girl."

"Oh, I didn't know that the Amish had rules about girls going to college and stuff," Felix said.

"A doctor," Clara said, shaking her head. "Imagine that. A woman doctor."

"Doctor Finigan is a woman!" Maisie said, still more irritated.

Clara considered that. "Well," she said slowly, "my Great-Aunt Martha served the town of Hallowell, Maine, as a midwife for over thirty years—"

"Mom used a midwife," Felix said, eager to show the girl that he wasn't as mean as his sister. Something about Clara interested him.

"Except she couldn't use her because twins are high risk," Maisie corrected.

Clara's eyes widened. "Twins? I've never seen twins before! Aunt Martha has told me about such a thing, two babies born at the same time—"

"Uh, yeah," Maisie said. "I guess all great-aunts are rocket scientists." She turned her back on Felix and Clara and went to peer out the open barn door.

"Rock what?" Clara said.

"Oh, don't pay attention to her. She's just crabby

because we landed so close to home," Felix said. "See, we went to the other Amish country, the one in Pennsylvania, a few years ago, and we were hoping for something a little more exciting." He grinned at her. "You don't have any idea what I'm talking about, do you?"

Clara blushed again. "I'm afraid not," she said. "Your language is so similar to mine, yet so different." She frowned, concentrating, then broke into a smile. "Of course!" she said. "You must be from England, and you speak the King's English. There are still people around here who speak it."

"King's English," Felix repeated. He called to his sister. "Maisie?"

"The thing is," Maisie answered, without moving, "I don't see any telephone wires at all. And wouldn't you think that even off in the distance there would be a tower or electric poles or something?"

Forgetting his arm for a moment, Felix propped himself up to get a better look out the door. Immediately, pain shot through him, and he let out another yelp, falling back onto the ground.

"There, there," Clara soothed. "I warned you to be still."

All Felix could do was hold his breath and wait for the pain to subside.

"I have three years' experience with caring for

someone sick," Clara said softly. "I did everything
the doctors told me to do for David. Everything. I
hardly left his side. Oh, his case grew desperate."
She shook her head. "Why, I even administered
those loathsome crawling leeches."

"Leeches!" Felix gasped.

Clara nodded. "Of course. His fever came
from too much blood. But even the bloodletting
didn't work."

Maisie was starting to feel like they were in a
horror movie instead of Amish country. "If you
could just point us in the direction of the first
town that isn't Amish?" she said.

"There," Clara said. "You've just said one of
those odd words again." She studied Felix with
great curiosity. "If you've come from Rhode
Island, where's your horse then?"

"Yeah, Maisie," Felix said. "Where's our horse?"

Maisie ignored him. Instead, she took a few
steps outside of the open barn door. Felix watched
her as she stood, hands on her hips, and took
stock of whatever was out there. He tried to stay
calm. After all, they were only in Massachusetts,
the state immediately north of Rhode Island.
They could be back home at Elm Medona before
their mother even realized they'd left.

"If my mother wasn't feeling poorly, I'd bring

you inside the house," Clara was telling him. "But if you stay right here, I can go inside and make you a poultice. That will help your arm feel better."

Felix had read the word *poultice* in books, but he was fairly certain he had never actually heard anyone say it. He was completely certain he'd never had anyone offer to make him one.

"You mean like with water and cloth and mustard or something?" he said, just to be sure he'd understood her right. Even though she was speaking English, she had a funny accent, like someone in a play.

"Onions," Clara said matter-of-factly as she got up. "Now don't move," she said, pointing at him. "After all that time taking care of David, I think I know what's best."

With that, she strode off, right across the barn and out the door where Maisie had been standing just a minute ago. Felix blinked hard.

"Maisie?" he called.

He stared out at the wide open space beyond the door. But all he saw was bright-blue sky, green pastures, and Clara walking away.

"Maisie?" he called again, even though he knew that his sister was gone.

· CHAPTER NINE ·

September 5

The air smelled different. That was the first thing Maisie thought as she walked across the pasture. She could actually smell grass and dirt and horse poop and smoke, each scent sharper and . . . she inhaled deeply, trying to find the word to describe what she meant. Cleaner, she decided. The air smelled cleaner. In New York, the air always had a hint of car fumes in it. On their block, the smell from the Laundromat hung in the air and food smells from nearby restaurants mixed with it. Since they moved to Newport, her mother had made a big show of taking exaggerated deep breaths and saying "Ah! *The salty sea air.*" But Maisie never really got a whiff of it. Sure, everything stayed kind of damp from being so close to the ocean, and once in a while a strong odor of seaweed infiltrated the air.

But here it was as if every scent was making itself known. Maisie paused. Like right now she could smell something strong and floral. Sure enough, a cluster of flowers appeared around a bend. Maisie kept walking and breathing in all the smells, keeping her eyes peeled for some sign of civilization.

A new smell. Maisie inhaled. Berries, just like the Union Square farmers' market on a hot summer day. Sure enough, she saw a tangle of blackberry bushes. The berries were bigger than any she'd seen before, even bigger than the ones her mother liked to buy at her favorite supermarket, Fairway, where the produce and meat and just about everything was superbig and shiny. Her stomach grumbled at the sight of so many berries, and Maisie realized she hadn't eaten anything since that mac and cheese.

She plucked a blackberry from its branch and popped it in her mouth. The flavor—intense and sweet and more blackberryish than any blackberry she'd ever tasted—exploded on her tongue. And the bushes were crowded with blackberries. Maisie decided to help herself. She chose the fullest bush, placed herself in front of it, and began to eat. Each berry tasted better than the one just before it, all of them plump, juicy, and slightly warm. *What kind of chemicals do these Bartons use that make the blackberries so delicious?* she wondered.

As soon as she wondered that, Maisie said, "Uh-oh."

She stepped away from the bush and turned slowly in every direction. Everything smelled clean, she realized, because it *was* clean. There was absolutely no pollution here. And she couldn't see any power lines anywhere because there *weren't* any power lines. And these blackberries were so good because they were, well, *real* blackberries, without Miracle-Gro or anything at all.

Maisie had figured out *where* they had landed. But *when* was it?

For the first time in her life, Maisie wished she'd paid a little more attention to her social studies teacher, Mrs. Johnson. All last year, Mrs. Johnson had taught them about American history—pilgrims and pioneers and settlers. Which group did Clara Barton fit into?

Pilgrims. She was fairly sure they wore shoes with big buckles. And they lived in Massachusetts. But didn't they live by the sea? No, Clara was not a pilgrim, Maisie decided with a certain measure of doubt.

All those Laura Ingalls Wilder books her
mother had loved as a girl and tried to get Maisie
to love took place somewhere out west, not here
in New England. So they hadn't landed back
when pioneers settled, whenever that was. Maisie
rubbed her temples as if that would help her
figure this out.

Wait a minute, Maisie thought. *Who cares what year
it is?* She'd find that out eventually. What really
mattered was that somehow she and Felix *had*
gone back in time. They were not in the twenty-
first century. They were not in Newport, Rhode
Island. A shiver of excitement spread through
her. Just yesterday, her life had seemed dull
and claustrophobic. She'd been stuck in a hot
apartment with no friends and her father halfway
around the world. And today? Well, today
everything was different.

Maisie stretched out on her back in the
sweet-smelling grass and stared up happily at
the bluest, clearest sky she'd ever seen. The taste
of blackberries lingered on her lips, and from
somewhere nearby, she could smell the musky
scent of horses mingling with the rich earth
and grass smells. Maybe they hadn't traveled
somewhere superexciting, but lying there, Maisie
felt happy to be out of Newport.

Clara Barton, Maisie thought, tucking her hands beneath her head. *Why in the world had they landed in Clara Barton's barn?*

"This is disgusting," Felix told Clara as she put the onion poultice on his arm.

"How would you ever tolerate leeches if you can't endure the strong smell of onions?" Clara said.

"Please stop talking about leeches." Felix groaned. "Besides, no one does anything like that anymore."

She looked at him, surprised.

"That's what they did in the olden days," Felix continued, "before antibiotics and stuff."

He heard his own words come out of his mouth and something settled in his chest. *The olden days.*

"You're not Amish, are you?" Felix said softly.

Clara shook her head. "I have to admit," she said, "I don't know what Amish is."

He studied her—the bonnet, the apron, the long dress, and the funny boots.

"Do you know the date today?" he asked, his mouth turning dry.

She smiled. "September fifth," she said.

Felix swallowed hard. It had been September 5 when he woke up in Newport this morning.

"Um," he said. "September fifth . . . ?"

"1836," Clara said.

"1836," Felix said. He did some subtraction and began shivering.

It was September 5, more than one hundred and seventy-five years earlier than it was supposed to be.

"1836," Felix repeated as if by saying it again it might change.

"Yes," Clara said.

Felix tried to concentrate. Had anything terrible happened in 1836? Anything catastrophic? He could feel his heart banging around under his ribs.

"We're not at war or anything, right?" he asked. *When was the Civil War?* he wondered. *Eighteen something.*

"I don't think so," Clara said.

"I mean, the North and the South get along and everything?"

"North and south what?"

"Of America?" Felix said.

Clara placed the back of her cool hand on his forehead and kept it there for a while until she announced, "No fever. When David's fevers came, he often spoke nonsense."

A great surge of compassion filled Felix. How could he tell this girl that some time, maybe some time soon, a terrible and bloody war would start and that her country would be divided by it? How could

he tell her that President Lincoln would be killed
and that slaves would be freed? And what about the
countless other historical moments that lay ahead?

Again he struggled to remember when the
Civil War began. Felix thought of all the times
Mrs. Johnson told him that someday he would
realize how important it was to know history. He
had no idea that day would come so soon.

"Is Abraham Lincoln the president?" Felix
asked Clara.

"The president—"

"Of the United States."

"You don't even know who our president is?"
Clara said sadly.

Felix shook his head. Maybe the Civil War was
a long way from now.

"For your information," Clara said, "Mr. Andrew
Jackson is the president of the United States."

Felix tried not to laugh. He had never even heard
of Andrew Jackson. *That guy won't do anything very special,* he
wanted to tell Clara. *No one will even remember him in a couple
hundred years.*

"Old Hickory himself," Clara said proudly.

"Old Hickory," Felix repeated, searching his
brain for some memory of this guy.

"He defeated the Red Stick Creeks at the Battle
of Horseshoe Bend," she said, excited. "My father

voted for him in both elections. He's completely paid off the national debt—"

"And this president . . . Jackson?"

She nodded.

"He's the . . . twelfth or thirteenth president?"

Clara laughed. "Andrew Jackson is the seventh president of the United States. He used to have John C. Calhoun as his vice president but—"

"That's all right," Felix interrupted.

Clara blushed. "I can recite the name of every general, captain, colonel, and sergeant, and I know the name of everyone from the president and cabinet to all the leading government officers by heart."

"Wow," Felix said, impressed. He certainly couldn't do that.

"But do you know what I used to think?" Clara said with a laugh. "I had no idea that they were all regular men. I thought they must certainly be larger than life, you know? I imagined the president might be as large as the meeting house, and the vice president as large as, oh, I don't know. A schoolhouse maybe."

Felix laughed. "I know what you mean," he said. "Last year I saw Johan Santana on the street, and I was shocked that he was so ordinary-looking in person."

"Johan—"

"Santana! Only the best pitcher in the game of baseball!" Felix said.

Clara frowned. "I don't know that game," she said.

"You don't know what baseball is?"

Clara shook her head.

"It's only the most amazing game ever," Felix said.

He couldn't believe it. Baseball hadn't been invented yet? He tried to remember when the first baseball game had been played, but he had no idea. That was the exact kind of thing his father would know without even looking it up.

"What's wrong?" Clara asked gently. "You suddenly looked so sad."

"I was just thinking about my father. He knows just about everything. He probably even knows all about Old Hickory and even that John Calhoun guy."

"My father, too! He's Captain Stephen Barton, and he fought in the Indian Wars, just like President Jackson," Clara said. "Except he fought in Ohio and Michigan. And his father fought under General Mad Anthony Wayne in the Revolutionary War. Why, you should hear his war stories!"

Felix nodded politely. "That would be great," he said. But what he was actually thinking about was how there could have been a war he had never even heard of before. Felix sighed. "Any sign of my sister out there?" he asked.

Clara looked out the barn door. "No. I suppose she went searching for that thing she needs so badly. What did she call it?"

"A phone," Felix said.

No matter how long or hard Maisie looked, she was not going to find a phone here in 1836.

They fell into an uncomfortable silence.

Then Clara said, "Do you know *The Lady of the Lake*?"

"Who's she?" Felix said.

Clara looked disappointed. "The book by Walter Scott?"

"What's it about?"

"Well," Clara said, "the poem's about the struggle between King James the Fifth and the powerful clan Douglas."

"Wait. It's a poem?"

"Yes," Clara said.

"I thought it was a book," Felix said.

"It's both," Clara explained.

"I've never heard of a poem long enough to be an entire book."

Clara laughed. "Even more reason to read it then."

"Maybe so," Felix said, intrigued. "You were

saying: There's a king and a powerful clan . . ."

"Yes, but at the very beginning of the poem, a mysterious knight called James Fitz-James arrives at the castle. This is important to know because soon enough he falls in love with Ellen, James of Douglas's daughter."

Felix listened as Clara told him the details of the story. He liked how excited she looked as she talked. That was how he felt about good stories, too.

"Oh, it's all very exciting," Clara said breathlessly. "But I shouldn't say any more. You must read it yourself to see how it all turns out."

"That does sound good," Felix said. "I'll have to get it when I get home," he added to be kind. He doubted a book that old was still in print.

"What are your favorite kinds of stories?" Clara asked him.

"I like just about everything. Spy stories and science fiction and *Harry Potter*." He stopped when he saw that confused look cross her face again. "All kinds of stories," he said.

"It's your turn to tell me a story now," Clara said. She adjusted her long dress and leaned back, her face expectant.

"I can't really think of any," Felix said.

"Do you know any war stories?" she asked. "You must."

"Well," he said slowly, "once I read about a war where Americans fought other Americans."

"Like the Loyalists and the Rebels?" Clara said.

"Uh, I don't think so," Felix said. Was there still another war he'd never heard of? Here he was, an American, and all these soldiers had died, and he didn't know what they had been fighting for.

"So, not a Revolutionary War story?"

Bingo! He knew about *that* war. "No," Felix said. "This isn't a real war." *Not yet, anyway*, he thought.

"So it's just a story. Like *The Lady of the Lake*."

"Sort of. In this story, people who live in the South want to start their own country. They want their own laws and their own president and everything."

"That's silly, isn't it?"

"No, Clara," Felix said. "It's very serious. They call it the bloodiest war of all time. And states are forced to take sides, to be either Union or Confederates." Like all historical facts, the details were a bit fuzzy to Felix. He hoped he was getting it mostly right.

"Which side does Massachusetts choose in this story?"

"Union," Felix said. "They want to keep the country unified."

"Good old Massachusetts," Clara said. "Then what?"

"Well, one of the things they're fighting over is

whether it should be legal to have slaves—"

"They had a war over that?" Clara said, surprised. "Does it end happily?"

Felix thought about that. "Yes, I think it does. Ultimately. But only after a lot of people die."

"That's what happens in war, though, isn't it?" Clara said matter-of-factly. She sighed. "Even so, I wish I could be a soldier."

"No, you don't, Clara. You don't want to be on a battlefield."

"Don't look so worried," she said, laughing at him. "Girls can't be soldiers, either, can they?"

She lifted the poultice from his arm. "How is your arm feeling now?"

He moved it cautiously. The sharp pain had subsided to a dull ache. "A little better," he said.

Clara placed the poultice back on his arm.

"Thanks," Felix said.

"Ugh! What's that awful smell?" Maisie asked. She was standing in the doorway of the barn, scowling.

"It's my poultice," Felix said.

"What's it made out of? Onions?" Maisie said, holding her hand over her nose as she walked toward him.

"Did you find your—?" Clara asked politely.

"Oh, no," Maisie said, looking directly at Felix. "There are no phones here."

"No kidding," Felix said.

"I mean, we traveled a long, long way from home," Maisie said.

"I know."

"No, Felix, I mean a *long, long, long* way."

"Maisie?" Felix said. "You'd better sit down." He'd always wanted to say that to somebody like they do in movies, and this seemed like the perfect time.

"You know, then?" she said, unable to hide her disappointment over not being the one to figure it out first.

"Maisie," Felix said, "it's September fifth—"

"Okay . . . ," she said.

"1836."

Felix and Maisie looked at each other for a long time. They could feel Clara watching them.

"1836," Maisie finally managed to say. "That's, like, after the Revolutionary War?"

"And before the Civil War," Felix said.

Clara had gotten to her feet and now loomed over them. "I don't mean to be rude," she said, "but what ever are you two talking about? And you never did tell me why you are in my barn."

"I know how we got here," Maisie said to Felix. "But I have no idea how in the world we're ever going to get back."

·CHAPTER TEN·

The Baseball Game

"Clara," Felix said, "where exactly are we?"

"On Captain Stephen Barton's farm," she answered tentatively.

"And where is Captain Stephen Barton's farm?" Maisie said, pacing in front of them.

"Oxford," Clara said. Then she added, "Massachusetts."

Maisie paused in her pacing just long enough to say, "I have no idea where Oxford is. I don't have any idea where anything in Massachusetts is."

"What does it matter?" Felix said miserably. "*Where* we are isn't quite as important as *when* we are, is it?"

His sister broke into a grin as if he had said

something wonderful. "That's right, bro," she said, suddenly cheerful.

"Huh?" Felix said. He certainly didn't feel any better. In fact, all he wanted was to be back in Newport, in his bed with his iPod on, and listening to the playlist his father had made for him before he'd gone off to Qatar.

"Well," Maisie said, her eyes twinkling, "we're here, right? We might as well make the most of it. I mean, we'll never have an opportunity like this again, will we?"

Clara got to her feet and swept her hand over her dress, wiping off the straw that clung to it. "You two are just the oddest people I've ever come across," she said.

"You have no idea what it's like here," Felix told Maisie. "They don't even have baseball yet."

Maisie grinned. "That's where we'll start then," she said. "We'll teach Clara Barton here how to play baseball."

"They probably don't even have balls," Felix mumbled.

Clara put her hands on her hips. "We most certainly do," she said. "And I can throw one with an under swing better than any boy's and make it go exactly where I intend it to."

"We'll see about that," Maisie said. She

couldn't help but think that a girl who had never heard of baseball couldn't play better than two kids whose father had spent countless warm Saturday afternoons in the park teaching them to throw and hit balls.

Clara laughed. "You've never had my brother David teach you anything."

Maisie started to look for something to use as a bat. She picked up and then rejected a pitchfork, a hoe, and a shovel. All too heavy or misshapen.

"Clara," Felix said softly. "I think you're going to be a good baseball player. There's one player called a pitcher whose job is just to throw the ball, and it sounds like you'd be perfect for that."

"But how can you play with that arm of yours?" Clara said, kneeling beside him.

"I forgot all about it!" Felix said, surprised. "This thing must really be working."

He watched Clara carefully remove the poultice from his arm.

"I had quite a skating accident myself a couple of years ago," Clara said as she poked and prodded his arm.

"You really are a tomboy," Felix said, unable to hide his admiration.

"There you go again with your funny words," Clara said. "A tomboy?"

"A girl who can do things like throw underhanded and skate superfast," Felix said.

"That's me, all right!" Clara said, blushing. "I felt so proud when I heard the surgeon say to my father, 'That was a hard case, Captain, but she stood it like a soldier.'" Clara patted Felix's arm. "And I can say the same to you, Felix. You stood it like a soldier."

Felix bent his arm carefully. "I think I'm good to go," he said.

From one corner of the barn came a loud clattering of metal and then a triumphant "aha!" from Maisie.

She appeared in front of Felix and Clara wielding a wooden stick.

"Baseball, anyone?" she said.

For the first time since he'd landed in the Barton's barn, Felix stepped outside. It was a bright, sunny day, and the smell of grass and flowers was strong. Though not stronger than the smell of farm animals. Felix wrinkled his nose.

"Do you have cows or something?" he said.

"Twenty-five milk cows," Clara said proudly.

"Watch where you step," Maisie said.

"And Highlanders, Virginians, and Morgans," Clara added.

When she saw the blank looks on Maisie's and Felix's faces, she said, "Horses! My father raises them."

Felix looked around. The farm was enormous, with two barns in addition to the one they'd been in, rolling hills in the distance, a pond, and a large house with porches and a balcony.

"We moved here when I was eight, after my uncle died," Clara explained. "It's three hundred acres with lots of grassland for the horses and room for my cousins to come and stay during the summer. They just left a few days ago, which is too bad. They would have liked to learn this baseball, too."

Maisie gave a low whistle. "Central Park is eight hundred acres," she said. "Two hundred and fifty of that is lawns, which means you live on a farm about as big as all the grass in Central Park." She patted her fleece vest.

"Maisie likes numbers," Felix explained. "She likes math, and I like reading."

"I'm the one who keeps all the stats for the Mets every season," Maisie said. "Well, usually."

The truth was she did it with her father, carefully filling in all the blanks in the Mets record book they got every opening day. Except this year.

"Our father moved to Qatar," Felix blurted out. "Nothing is the same anymore."

Maisie took in all of the things around them:

the barn, the rolling hills, Clara herself. She smiled. *Nothing is the same anymore at all,* she thought excitedly. She walked ahead of them up a hill in search of a flat area to play baseball.

Felix watched his sister disappear over the crest.

"Your father moved away?" Clara asked. "Without you?"

Felix sighed. Being in 1836 was hard enough without having to explain his parents' divorce.

"It's complicated," he said.

"Over here!" Maisie called to them.

Relieved, Felix ran toward her voice. Clara ran alongside him, then hitched up her skirt and took off ahead of him.

"Hurry up," she said, glancing over her shoulder before she, too, disappeared over the crest of the hill.

"Maybe you guys can find something to use for bases!" Maisie said.

She watched as Felix and Clara ran around the fields searching for things to use as bases and home plate. Why, she wondered, did Felix always manage to make friends so easily while she seemed to offend people? Even in a different century he was able to connect with someone who he didn't—couldn't!—have anything in common with.

She sighed and dropped onto the warm grass,

unzipping her fleece and using it as a pillow
beneath her head. The sun shone high in the
sky now, directly overhead. Noon. Her mother
was probably breaking for lunch in her office on
Thames Street back in Newport. Maisie could
imagine her turning off her computer and taking
out her egg salad sandwich and banana from her
lunch bag.

Felix's laughter floated around Maisie, mixing
in with the lazy buzz of a bee. *Fine,* she thought.
*Be friends with a person who's, like, two hundred years old,
technically.* Thinking how old Clara would be felt
too creepy. Maisie sat up quickly. What would
Clara think about computers? She'd never heard
of anything like them, that was for sure. Maybe
she'd never even heard of egg salad sandwiches.
Even sandwiches had to get invented, right?

Clara had her arms full of leaves, and she and
Felix were running toward Maisie now.

No baseball, Maisie thought as she watched them.
No phones. No divorce. Deep inside, Maisie's chest
fluttered. An idea was taking shape, an incredible
idea. A brilliant idea. *What if we didn't go back?*
Maisie wondered. *What if we stayed right here on
Captain Stephen Barton's farm in 1836?*

As Felix explained the game to Clara, he was
impressed with how quickly she caught on. *Back*

home, he thought, and then he caught himself and changed to *back in New York,* he'd played on a Little League team, the Knights, made up of boys and girls. Charlotte Weinberg was the team's best player. Once she even pitched a no-hitter. Maisie liked to tease him and call Charlotte his girlfriend. Deep down, Felix didn't mind that at all. Every time he stood close to Charlotte, even when she was all sweaty from running, he felt a little dizzy. She had strawberry-blond hair that practically shined in the sunlight and just enough freckles to make her perfect.

"So," Clara was saying, "I throw the ball to Maisie, aiming so she thinks she can hit it, but hoping she misses. And that's called a strike. Three strikes and her turn is finished."

"Three strikes and she's out," Felix corrected her. "Which is the same as being finished."

"Three outs and we change places," Clara said.

"Right," Felix said. "Really baseball teams have nine people, of course," he said, suddenly crabby. He would probably never see Charlotte Weinberg again. Or any of the Knights, for that matter. Even if they did manage to get back to the twenty-first century.

"It's a pity my cousins have all left," Clara said. "They're always ready for adventures."

Felix saw something in Clara's face then.

Something he recognized. She was lonely.

"Who needs them?" he said, marking off first base with a pile of leaves. "We'll do just fine."

Clara grinned at him. "Yes, we will," she said. "How does that arm feel?"

He rubbed the spot that still vaguely hurt. "Sore, but better," he said. Felix grinned at her. "I didn't want you coming at me with those leeches," he said.

By the time they were finished laying out the bases, they still had more leaves left over. Felix couldn't resist. He took a big handful from Clara and tossed them right at her. They landed in her hair and on her shoulders.

"Oh!" she cried, startled.

But then something gleamed in her dark eyes, and Felix knew to run, fast. He wasn't fast enough for Clara, though. She caught him easily and knocked him to the ground, where she held him down by his good arm and deposited the rest of the leaves and twigs right in his face.

"You win!" Felix said, laughing and spitting out bits of grass.

"See?" Clara said, releasing him. "Wouldn't I make a very good soldier?"

"I think you would, Clara," Felix said seriously. His stomach felt all caught up in knots as he

realized that Clara Barton would go on to live
an entire life, a life that began and ended long
before he was even born. Maybe she actually
did become a soldier. Maybe she . . . he stopped
himself from thinking any more on the topic.

"Don't look so glum," Clara said, tossing a few
leaves back at him.

Felix surprised himself by grabbing her and
giving her a good, hard hug. He surprised Clara,
too. She squirmed out of his arms and stepped
back awkwardly.

"Whatever was that for?"

"I . . . I . . ." But how could he explain his
feelings to her when *he* couldn't even understand
them?

"It's just that," he began, "that being a soldier
is so dangerous."

Clara laughed. "*Pshaw!* It's exciting. And noble."

"Like your knights in *The Lady of the Lake*?"
Felix said.

"Yes! Like that. And like my father, of course."
She studied his face a moment. "Wasn't your father
in the war?" she asked.

Felix shook his head.

"Hey!" Maisie shouted. "Are we ever going to
play ball? Or are you two running off to get married
or something?"

Clara looked horrified.

"No, no," Felix told Clara quickly. "She's just teasing me. She does that all the time."

"I don't think it's funny," Clara said, stomping away from him toward what they'd marked as the pitcher's mound. "Not at all."

"Play ball!" Felix called from the outfield.

Clara turned on the pitcher's mound to face him.

"That's what we say to start the game," Felix called out to Clara. "Now remember what I taught you."

Clara turned and met Maisie's eyes. Then she wound up and let the ball fly to Maisie, underhanded.

"Sta-rike!" Felix called.

Maisie took a step back to catch her breath. "Wow!" she said. "Nice arm!"

Clara didn't acknowledge her at all. She just wound up again and pitched, hard.

"Sta—" Felix called.

"I know!" Maisie interrupted him.

She glared at Clara. Clara smiled back at her.

"Sure. She's never played baseball before," Maisie muttered.

This time the pitch went into the grass, exploding at Maisie's feet. Felix explained to Clara that that was called a "ball" and that Maisie got another turn.

Clara's next pitch was perfect. Maisie smacked it out into left field where it dropped right into Felix's waiting hands.

"She's out, right?" Clara asked Felix.

"This baseball is a wonderful game," Clara said after they'd each taken several turns at bat. "I can't wait to teach everyone."

The three of them walked down the hill toward the well behind the house. The idea of a well excited Felix. It was like something from a novel or an old movie.

"You should see it when two entire teams play," Maisie said. "Like out at Shea Stadium when the lights come on and the field is almost a fake green."

Felix grinned. Shea Stadium had been replaced by Citi Field a couple of years earlier. Last Christmas, their father had given them both T-shirts that said: IT'S STILL SHEA TO ME. Going to Shea Stadium meant taking the subway all the way out to Queens after school. It meant hot dogs and giant sodas and pretzels with mustard. It meant their parents weren't divorced.

"You mean the game is played at night?" Clara said.

"Sometimes," Maisie said. "Oh," she added, realizing what Clara must be thinking, "they can light the field. It's . . . um . . . complicated."

Up ahead, Felix saw the well. It looked just like he'd hoped it would. A wooden box, painted white, with a kind of roof above it and a silver bucket on a pulley.

"Look at this," he said excitedly, cranking the handle to send the bucket down into the well.

Clara laughed. "You are the most peculiar boy I've ever met," she said.

The bucket made a splash when it hit the water. Felix lowered it even farther, then brought it up, water sloshing as it came back to the surface.

Clara took a big ladle from the side of the well and dipped it into the bucket, offering it first to Maisie, who took a big drink.

"That's . . . delicious," she said, drinking some more.

She handed the ladle to Felix. "I guess we've never really had such pure water," he said after drinking two ladlefuls himself.

Clara took her turn, staring at them over the ladle as she drank.

"But it's not just the water," Maisie said. "It's the blackberries and the air and everything. Everything here is just better."

"Maisie," Felix said, feeling panic rising in his gut. "We *are* going back. You know that, right?"

"Back to what? That crummy, stuffy apartment? Life without Dad?"

"Dad will come home for Christmas. He said so."

"You can go back if you want," Maisie said. "But I might just stay here."

Clara cleared her throat. "Well, you two can stay the night and decide when to go home tomorrow," she said in her soft voice. "We have lots of extra beds in the attic."

"That's a great idea," Maisie said quickly. She even remembered to add, "Thanks, Clara."

"Thanks," Clara repeated. Then she said it again. "Thanks."

"It's like shorthand, you know?" Maisie said. "For *thank you*."

"Shorthand," Clara repeated. "Curious word," she said to herself. Then, as if she remembered Maisie and Felix, she said, "Why don't I go inside and see what there is for supper?"

She began to walk in the direction of the side door of the house, but when she realized Maisie and Felix were following her, Clara stopped.

"I don't mean to be ungracious," she said carefully. "But maybe you should wait outside. How ever could I explain who you are to my family? What will they say if I tell them I found you in the barn?"

"But I thought you said we could sleep in the attic?" Felix said. He didn't like the idea of staying at all. But staying in the barn sounded even worse.

"Yes! Of course! But I'll sneak you up the back stairs after dark."

"This is so exciting," Maisie said.

"I'll be right back," Clara told them. "Wait here."

"We have to go home," Felix said.

"I thought you'd like to hang around longer," Maisie said. "With your new girlfriend."

"Oh stop," Felix said, dropping onto the grass. "Don't pick on me just because Clara likes me better."

"She does not!" Maisie said.

The sun had started to set, and the air was turning cooler. Felix wished he had on long pants and his own warm fleece rather than a T-shirt and shorts. He could practically picture them in his room back home.

"Let's not fight, Maisie," Felix said. Goose bumps traveled up his arms. "Let's just try to figure out how to get back."

Maisie took a deep breath. "Tomorrow," she said. "I promise. For tonight, let's just enjoy 1836."

They sat on the grass in silence for a moment.

"It is so quiet here," Felix said.

"I like it," Maisie said.

Felix sighed. "It's nice," he admitted. Then he added, "For one night."

Maisie patted his knee. "Right," she said, grinning to herself.

It seemed to Felix that they waited hours and hours before Clara finally reemerged carrying a picnic basket. He was so hungry by then that he thought he might eat almost anything. But still he watched her approaching with some trepidation. Felix was a fussy eater. He didn't like tuna fish or mayonnaise or things that were too crunchy. He liked tomatoes, but only if they were cooked. He didn't like runny eggs, either. Maisie, on the other hand, liked everything. Curry, sushi, capers. For all he knew, everything was crunchy or made with raw tomatoes and runny eggs in 1836.

"Sorry that took so long," Clara was saying as she spread a quilt on the grass. "I didn't want to rouse suspicions."

She opened the basket and set two china plates on the quilt. They were blue and white with some kind of picture of trees and things on them. Next, she took out heavy, silver forks and knives that looked like they were from a scary slasher movie. She placed the silverware on two floral, cotton napkins.

"Fancy," Maisie said.

"You didn't think I was going to make you eat with your hands, did you?" Clara said.

"We just use paper plates and plastic forks on picnics," Maisie said. "That's all."

Clara burst out laughing. "*Paper* plates?" she managed. "If you put hot food on *paper*, it would fall right through. Honestly!"

Of course, Felix realized. Things like paper plates and anything made out of plastic weren't invented yet. He didn't like how excited Maisie looked as she realized the exact same thing. The more she grew intrigued by things here, the less likely she would be to help him figure out how to get back home.

"You must spend a lot of time washing dishes and stuff," Felix said. Maisie hated doing kitchen chores. That should make her think twice about going back on their deal and trying to stay here instead of going home.

"You are the oddest boy ever," Clara said, still chuckling. She continued to unpack the basket, laying out bowls of steaming food.

String beans. Asparagus. *Phew!* Felix thought. Not only did he recognize them, but they looked nicely overcooked. Sliced potatoes, also mushy. Some kind of meat with bright green peas. *Nothing crunchy so far,* Felix thought as he peered at the contents of the last bowl.

"What in the world?" he said softly.

"Are those hooves?" Maisie shrieked.

Clara looked baffled. "Calves' hooves," she said.

"Calves' feet?" Felix asked.

"You eat them?" Maisie said. Even though she liked sushi and other things that some kids didn't want to eat, she drew the line at hooves.

"Don't you?" Clara said.

"Uh. No."

Surprisingly, Clara brightened. "I'm also a vegetarian," she said. "I haven't eaten meat since the day I saw some farm hands struggling to get a large, red ox into the barn."

Felix liked the idea of an ox. Like the well, an ox was something straight out of a novel. He tried to picture what one looked like exactly but could come up with only a cartoon version. Still, he was happy to have the distraction from those hooves, which appeared to have some kind of jelly on them.

"They finally did get him inside, and then one of them raised an ax high in the air and struck him here." Clara rubbed the back of her neck. "The ox fell, and I fainted!" Clara blushed deep red, remembering. "When I opened my eyes and remembered what I had seen in the barn, I began to cry. From that day on, I lost any desire for meat."

"Yes!" Maisie said. "Exactly! I've lost my desire for meat."

Clara seemed to consider this.

"Everything looks great," Felix told Clara, who was unwrapping a napkin with cornbread tucked inside. He touched her arm. "Thank you for all this."

"Well," Clara said, smoothing her skirt. "You are welcome."

Maisie had started to fill her plate with food—except the hooves. She sniffed each thing, frowning slightly. Felix didn't want to offend Clara, so he made a big show of saying how delicious everything looked, how string beans were his absolute favorite, and how the smells were making him even hungrier.

To be polite, Maisie pierced a piece of meat with her fork and studied it. If Clara's family ate feet, Maisie couldn't imagine what this was.

As if she read Maisie's mind, Clara said, "Lamb."

"I love lamb," Felix said, scooping some onto his plate.

What a liar! Maisie thought. Felix cried once when their mother made a leg of lamb. At least *that* had been marinated in spices and grilled. This lamb had a greasy, stringy quality to it. If Maisie hadn't been so hungry, she wouldn't have even tasted it. But she had no choice, did she? She didn't want to be rude.

She bit the piece of her meat, and immediately the taste of something wild and gamey filled her mouth. As she chewed, the meat seemed to get bigger instead of smaller. When she tried to swallow it, she gagged. It just wouldn't go down.

Felix took a great, big bite. Immediately his face twisted into disgust.

"Isn't it yummy?" Maisie said, forcing her piece down at last.

"Uh-huh," Felix said.

Maisie filled her mouth with the bland potatoes. But even they couldn't quite get rid of that taste of wild animal. Felix looked about as miserable as he could look. But he kept chewing the tough meat. When he saw Maisie smirking at him, he forced a smile at Clara just to bug his sister.

By the time they finished eating, the sky was turning a deep lavender. In the distance, the cows were making their way slowly over the hills toward home. Crickets began to sing, and an unfamiliar sense of serenity filled the evening air.

"Look!" Felix said.

Maisie followed where his finger pointed. The field was actually glowing with hundreds of flickering lights.

"Whoa!" cried Maisie. "We never see those anywhere besides Central Park."

"Fireflies?" Clara wondered softly.

"They're beautiful," Maisie said, her voice filled with wonder.

The three of them sat in silence, watching as the field grew thick with fireflies, their lights flickering like the twinkly white lights the Robbins family always put on their Christmas tree. Despite the vegetables being "boiled to death," as their father would say, the cornbread's texture was as grainy as sand, and the tough, gamey lamb that made her want to throw up, Maisie decided it would still be better here than back in Newport.

•CHAPTER ELEVEN•

Bedtime Stories

"Father," Clara said. "Will you tell me a story tonight?"

Maisie and Felix sat in the dark back stairway, waiting to hear one of Captain Stephen Barton's war stories. Clara had sneaked them in the back door and hurried them through the kitchen and into this stairway. Then she ordered them to be absolutely quiet and stay put. On the way, Felix glimpsed a large sitting room with lots of big windows looking out over the farm. At a desk sat Clara's father, a tall man with perfectly straight posture and a gray beard.

"Of course," they heard him say. His voice sounded weary and old. "Which story would you like tonight?"

284 1 4

"Tecumseh!" Clara said.

Her father laughed. "You've heard that one so many times, Clara. I don't want to bore you."

"You? Bore me?" Clara said. "Never!"

"I think the war stories interest you, not their narrator."

"No, no," Clara insisted. "Both the stories and the narrator interest me."

It was clear that this routine was a familiar one, and hearing it made Maisie miss her father. At night it had been his job to tell her and Felix bedtime stories. Even though they weren't war stories, they were good ones.

Maisie sighed and rested her head against Felix's knees. "War stories," she muttered.

"Sssshhh," Felix said softly.

There was the sound of someone walking around and then settling in a chair. Then the smell of pipe tobacco floated in the air.

"Our story begins in Indiana territory," Captain Barton said.

"Can you speak louder, Father?" Clara said in a loud voice herself.

"I don't want to wake anyone," he said.

"It's just . . . just that my ears are all cottony and—"

"Cottony ears?"

Felix stifled a laugh.

"Yes. Like there's cotton in them."

"All right then, our story begins in Indiana territory," Captain Barton said loudly.

He sighed and paused before he continued. "I was only twenty-one when I joined the recruits to fight the wars for the western frontiers. A boy, really. Just seven years older than you are now. We walked from Boston to Philadelphia and on to Michigan, which was the extreme western frontier and full of Indians. I served side by side with William Henry Harrison—"

"Old Tippecanoe himself!" Clara interrupted.

"Three years serving with him, Clara," her father said. His voice grew more solemn. "I remember lying in the tangled marshes of Michigan, helpless, so far from home. Having to drink muddy water, to eat animals— even dogs—that had died from starvation just to stay alive myself."

"I cannot imagine it," Clara said, her voice solemn, too. "I cannot imagine what you endured. Or the horrible things you saw. Tomahawks swung right over your head!"

"When I remember a feathered arrow quivering or the sound of musket fire, it makes me shudder. But it is because of what I and others like me endured that our country is so great. From these wild and dangerous scenes of suffering, this country as we know it sprung up."

"How you love this country," Clara said proudly.

"I do, yes," her father said, his voice cracking. "Now, I think the time has come for a certain young lady to go to bed."

"But you haven't even told me about Tecumseh or the walk back home through the wilderness of Ohio and New York or how you fell in love with the Mohawk and Genesee valleys or—"

"The stories will still be here tomorrow," her father said.

Clara gave an exaggerated yawn. "Time for bed," she said.

Felix and Maisie listened to the sounds of Clara and her father saying good night. It made Felix homesick, and he thought about his own bed, with the blankets arranged in just the right order, from lightest to heaviest. His mother always put a lavender-scented softener sheet in the dryer, and everything carried a hint of that scent. When he breathed deeply here, he smelled wax and oil and smoke, all unfamiliar and not at all comforting.

"It was a good story," Maisie admitted. "I guess."

"The thing is," Felix said, "it's all true. Tomahawks and eating dogs to survive and walking all the way to Michigan."

"It's like we stepped into a movie or something, isn't it?" Maisie said.

Felix didn't like the hint of excitement in her voice. "Don't sound so thrilled," he told her. "You know what's coming? The Civil War. And I have a feeling Clara Barton has something to do in it. That scroll we took from The Treasure Chest might be our clue."

"What could she possibly have to do with the Civil War?" Maisie said. "She's fourteen, only two years older than us."

"She won't be so young when the war happens," Felix reminded Maisie.

"That's true."

"We need to read that paper more carefully," he said.

"When we get upstairs alone," Maisie agreed.

Clara appeared at the bottom of the stairs and grinned up at them. "Wasn't that story marvelous?" she said proudly.

"You were right, Clara," Felix said. "I could listen to your father all night." He meant it, too.

Clara climbed the stairs to sit with them. "He was there at the slaying of Tecumseh, too," she said.

"How many states are there these days, anyway?" Maisie asked.

"You don't *know*?"

"I know there's going to be fifty—" Maisie began.

Felix yanked on her arm to make her shut up.

Clara frowned. "There are twenty-five," she said. "Arkansas was admitted in June."

And then to Felix's delight and Maisie's annoyance, she rattled off their names. Maisie liked to be the smartest kid around, and Clara was making her feel like maybe this time she wasn't. She was tempted to prove to Clara that she knew a lot of stuff, too. Like: Remember the name *Hawaii* because it's going to be the fiftieth state. Or: If you go to California right now, you can find some gold before anyone else gets there.

"Wow," Felix said. "I don't know if I could name all the states." All he could think about were all the states she hadn't named. *What is going on in California and Colorado and the other twenty-five states?* he wondered.

Maisie yawned and pointed up the stairs. "I'm guessing the attic is this way?" she said, and started to climb the steep steps.

"Yes," Clara said from behind her. "All the way up."

Maisie got to the top and stepped immediately into a large, open room with slanted ceilings and exposed beams and rafters. Four twin beds lined one wall, each covered in a faded quilt like the one they'd eaten their picnic on earlier.

Suddenly Maisie felt exhausted. She lay on the

bed closest to her, stretching her legs and looking up at the roughly hewn ceiling. The beams had slashes all across them, and Maisie realized she was seeing the actual ax marks left from cutting down trees. She sat up and reached her hand up and ran her fingers over them. When she did, a shiver crept up her back. Someone had chopped down this tree and built this house. She had never even thought about anyone doing such a thing before.

"Lucky that my cousins left and you can stay up here," Clara said. She fanned the air with her hands. "A bit airless," she said, and moved to the small windows above the beds to open them. "Like breathing through cotton."

"Cottony? Like your ears?" Felix teased.

Clara turned pink. "What a silly thing to say! But I wanted you to be able to hear, and I couldn't think of one earthly reason that he should speak louder when everyone was asleep already."

Cool air filled the room as soon as she opened all the windows, and Clara took a deep breath. "There," she said. "Better."

"Thanks, Clara," Felix said. "For getting us food and letting us stay and everything."

"Tomorrow we'll find your parents and make sure you get home safely," she said.

"Oh," Maisie said, "don't worry about that."

Clara yawned. "Well," she said. "Shall I bring you some buttermilk?"

"For what?" Maisie asked. To Maisie, buttermilk was the thing her mother put in pancakes and waffles.

"Why, to drink!" Clara said, exasperated.

"I don't think so," Felix said cautiously. He'd had enough new things for one day.

"All right then," Clara said. "Good night."

They watched her as she walked across the room and then disappeared down the stairs.

They sat on their beds quietly until they were certain she was gone.

Then Maisie said, "Okay, give me that piece of paper."

Felix blinked at her. "I don't have it. You have it."

"No, I don't! I specifically remember you having it."

They stared at each other. There was no point in saying anything more. The letter was missing. They sat quietly then—Felix worried, Maisie thrilled.

Felix woke to the strange sounds of a rooster crowing, cows mooing, and a horse neighing. The smells rising up from the kitchen, however, were completely familiar: bacon, eggs, and cornbread.

His stomach growled. And his chest felt tight with worry about where the letter had disappeared to.

What if they couldn't get back without it?

Maisie was still asleep in the bed beside him, her face scrunched up, her hands clenched into tight fists. The sight of her broke his heart. He had noticed she slept that way ever since their parents announced their divorce.

The attic door creaked open, and Clara walked in carrying two plates.

"Oh good," she said. "You're awake." She looked down at Maisie and said in a lower voice, "At least one of you is awake."

She handed a fork and a plate to Felix. Bacon, eggs, and cornbread.

He immediately started to eat. The bacon looked kind of weird, thicker and fattier than the Oscar Mayer they had at home. And the eggs looked weird, too, their yolks bigger and more yellow. But they weren't runny at all, and the taste was practically the same as the ones his mom made. Maybe even better.

Maisie groaned and rubbed her eyes. She stared at Felix hard, then at Clara harder. For a brief moment she looked confused, but then she broke into a huge grin.

"1836," she said.

"Breakfast," Clara said and held out the other plate and fork to Maisie.

"Thanks," Maisie said. "Nothing like room service."

"I should record these odd things you both say," Clara said. "Room service," she said, more to herself than to them, as if mulling over its meaning.

"In hotels," Felix began to explain. But then he stopped, because for room service you needed a telephone and probably an elevator and all sorts of things that did not exist yet. "When they bring your dinner or breakfast to your room," he said finally.

Clara brightened. "Hotels! Yes, I've heard about them. Father had a friend visiting us here who talked all about the Tremont Hotel in Boston," she began. But then she shook her head. "No, you won't even believe it."

"What?" Felix said.

"Well," Clara said, "according to this friend of father's—and he's a reputable source, truly he is—the Tremont Hotel has indoor plumbing and running water! Can you even imagine?" Clara paused as if she was trying to imagine it. "I have heard the Astor House in New York City that opened this year rivals it," she added.

Felix wondered if there were only two hotels in

the whole country. Well, all twenty-five states of the country.

"I wish you hadn't said that," Maisie said. "About indoor plumbing," she added, squirming.

"Oh," Clara said. "The chamber pot is beneath your bed."

Maisie frowned. She'd never heard the word before, but she didn't have to think too hard to understand what it was. She reached under the bed and pulled out a bowl with a handle and a red-and-white floral pattern. No wonder Clara thought indoor plumbing was such a unique thing to offer.

"Well," Maisie said, "are you two going to sit there and stare at me, or are you going to give me some privacy?"

"I vote for privacy," Felix said quickly. "I think I have to go to the barn and look for that thing we lost."

He and Clara headed for the stairs.

Behind him he heard Maisie groan. "You have got to be kidding me," she said. "A chamber pot?"

"Let's see," Felix said as he stood in the barn, trying to get his bearings. "I landed here, I think."

Clara watched him carefully. "Landed?" she said quietly.

"Uh . . ." He tried to think of an explanation,

but instead he just shrugged. "Landed," he said.

Clara's gaze swept upward, then down to the spot where indeed Felix had landed, and where he now was on his hands and knees searching.

"But how could you have even gotten up there?" she asked him.

Felix stopped searching long enough to say, "It's complicated."

"I can understand complicated things," Clara said.

"I know you can, Clara," Felix said. The paper didn't seem to be here. He sighed and sat cross-legged on the hay-strewn barn floor. "But I can't even begin to explain it myself."

She crossed her arms across her chest and waited.

"Maisie and I live in—"

"Rhode Island," she said. "I know that."

"We live in our great-great-grandfather's house. Well, sort of."

"Either you live there or you don't," Clara said, exasperated.

Felix took a deep breath and tried again. "We didn't want to come here exactly. It just sort of happened." He added to himself, "And that paper has something to do with it."

"You simply are talking nonsense!" Clara said. "Surely there is an explanation for how you came to be in my barn—"

From the doorway, Maisie's voice interrupted. "Did you find it?"

Felix was never so happy to have Maisie arrive and rescue him, something she'd done from time to time their entire lives. "It's not here," he said, getting to his feet. "Let's go and look in the field where we played baseball."

Maisie took off immediately, and Felix rushed to follow her. If they found that paper from The Treasure Chest, and he and Maisie each held on to it, Felix thought they would end up back at home, which is exactly where he wanted to be right now. He wondered if their mother had called the police. Had she called their father in Qatar? She must have been crying like crazy, certain they had run away or been abducted.

No matter what Maisie wanted or said or did, Felix intended to go home as soon as possible. And that paper was the way back. He hoped.

From the field, Maisie waved something in the air and shouted.

"I've got it!"

Relief filled Felix. Even if home was just that crummy apartment far from Bethune Street, he wanted to get there as soon as possible. He broke into a run. Clara had reached him and met him stride for stride.

"What's this piece of paper that's so important?" she asked him.

Felix realized it didn't matter what he told her. As soon as he reached Maisie, he would grab the paper and the two of them would be gone.

"Just something we need back home," he said, hoping that would satisfy her.

He sprinted ahead of her.

The sun was bright and hot, and the farm smells filled his nose. Behind Maisie, three horses stood eating grass, their coats shiny in the sunlight.

"You must have dropped it when you were running," Maisie said when he reached her.

Felix paused only long enough to take a quick look around. *Good-bye, 1836,* he thought. Clara was right behind him. *Good-bye, Clara Barton.*

He knew that if he explained to Maisie what he was about to do she would try to talk him out of it. Well, she would forgive him eventually.

"So what is this piece of paper that has caused so much trouble?" Clara said.

Maisie looked right at Felix. He looked back at her. Then he grabbed one end of the paper, just like he had back in The Treasure Chest.

"Good-bye, Clara!" he shouted. "Good luck!"

Felix closed his eyes and waited.

·CHAPTER TWELVE·

How Peculiar

"What are you doing?" Maisie said after an eternal moment.

Felix opened his eyes. His heart sank when he took in those rolling hills, the pond, the barn, the three houses, and Maisie and Clara staring at him. The paper was still in his hands, and Maisie still held one corner of it. But they had gone absolutely nowhere. How was this possible? He was certain he'd figured out how to get home.

"I thought . . . ," Felix began.

"You tried to get back, didn't you?" Maisie said. "Without even discussing it with me?"

Clara looked bewildered. "But how could you

go home from here?" she asked. "Did you intend on stealing one of our horses?"

As if he understood, the black horse lifted his head and neighed. "No, no," Felix said. "Nothing like that, Clara."

He took his sister's arm and pulled her away from Clara to talk in private.

"You said we would stay one night and then go back home."

"You tried to trick me," Maisie said.

"Because I knew you were going to keep stalling and stalling, and we'd never leave here," Felix said.

"I think somehow we came here to meet her," Maisie said thoughtfully. "I don't know why yet, but I don't want to leave before we figure it out."

"See?" Felix said. "You're stalling already."

"I'm not, really. Think about it. Why did we land *here* of all places? Why did Clara Barton find us in that barn? There must be a reason, Felix."

"Mom has probably called the police by now," he said. "She's probably worried sick."

"I'll make a deal with you—" Maisie began.

"No!" Felix said, louder than he intended.

From across the meadow, Clara looked over at them.

Lowering his voice, he said, "No more deals." He realized that Maisie had let go of her corner of the paper. He pulled it close to his chest.

"You go then," Maisie said. "Leave me here, and you go back."

"Without you?" Felix said.

"Please, Felix," she said, "just one more day. We'll figure out why we came here, and then we'll go back. I promise."

Despite his better judgment, Felix nodded.

"Thank you," Maisie said and gave him a big hug.

What Maisie didn't tell her brother was that she had thought the same thing he had: If they both held on to the paper at the same time, they would go back home. That was how they got here in the first place. Surely the same thing worked in reverse? But she and Felix had both grasped the paper and nothing had happened. They were still here on Clara Barton's farm in 1836. So how exactly were they going to get home?

"I will bring back our dinner," Clara said, getting them settled in the same place where they'd eaten the day before.

In 1836, *dinner* meant *lunch*. In the evening, you ate *supper*. Felix had figured that out yesterday, but it still sounded odd to him.

"Thanks, Clara," he said.

As soon as she left, Felix looked at Maisie and said firmly, "We need a plan."

Maisie surprised him by agreeing. "Let's look at the paper," she said. "I bet that's the key."

Maisie sat cross-legged on the grass, the paper open on her lap. "Dorence Atwater," she said finally, looking up at Felix. "Does that name ring a bell?

He shook his head.

"Do you know where Andersonville is?"

"Near here?" he guessed.

Maisie chewed her bottom lip and kept reading.

Impatient, Felix asked her, "Who is this Dorence Atwater? What does he have to do with Clara Barton? Or us for that matter?"

She didn't answer him.

"Maisie! Give me the letter and let me figure it out."

Slowly, Maisie lifted her head again and looked right into Felix's eyes. "It's just terrible," she managed to say.

"What? What is it?"

His sister handed the letter to Felix. "See for yourself," she said.

Felix read. The letter, written by Dorence Atwater, was addressed directly to Clara Barton!

Back in The Treasure Chest, they didn't have the time to make out the fancy writing.

"Maisie," Felix said, "I think this letter is for Clara. It says he copied this list of the dead Civil War soldiers in Andersonville, Georgia. And that he managed to get it out without being discovered by the Andersonville officials."

He continued to read some more, then told Maisie, "He took it with him through the enemy lines when he was released from there as a prisoner of war. Having been afraid that the names of the dead would never get to their families, it was his intention to publish it."

Now it was Felix's turn to look up from the letter.

"Maisie, this says that there are thirteen thousand names on this list," he said quietly.

Maisie gasped.

"And it's dated 1864," Felix said.

"That's thirty years from now," Maisie said.

"Andersonville was a prisoner of war camp during the Civil War," Felix said, pointing to the letter. He read from it, "'People are dying all around me. I can do nothing to save them, but I can let their families know exactly where they are buried—where to put flowers and pray.'"

"So this Atwater guy went to Clara Barton with this list he snuck out of the camp and asked her to help him notify their families?"

"I think so," Felix said.

"That's an awful lot of people," Maisie added.

The enormity of this settled around them as thick and heavy as the August humidity.

Clara came skipping toward them with the basket of food and the quilt. Watching her, a strange feeling came over both Maisie and Felix. Here was a young girl, young like they were. Yet in their hands they held a letter that told them that somehow she would be brought into the horrors of the Civil War. To what extent, they couldn't even guess. But the idea was overwhelming. Why did Dorence Atwater approach Clara Barton for help? Had she done something else during the war that made him believe she was the person to assist him? They couldn't help but think of their own futures. What paths would they travel in the next three decades? What mark would they make?

"Why do you two look so solemn?" Clara asked.

Unable to speak, Felix shrugged and carefully rolled up the letter. He wondered what would happen if he threw the thing away. Maybe that would save Clara from whatever horrors of war she might encounter. He wanted her to always be a shy and generous tomboy, pitching a ball on a late summer afternoon.

Maisie looked at Clara now as if she were seeing her for the first time.

"Clara," Maisie said, "I believe you are the type of person who would help anyone who came to your door for a favor, no matter how daunting or enormous that favor was."

"I think so," Clara said, after considering the question.

"Do you think that's your fate? To help others?" Maisie asked.

Felix looked at his sister in admiration. She was trying to piece together both the young Clara and the woman she would become.

"I do believe I would like to do that, yes. Nursing my brother these past few years brought me great satisfaction. My parents worry, though, that my shyness will prevent me from doing anything of much importance."

Impulsively, Maisie reached out to Clara, grabbing her hand. "Oh no, Clara!" she said emphatically. "I don't know exactly how or why, but I believe you will do something important. Maybe even many important things that will help thousands of people."

Clara squeezed Maisie's hand. "You are so peculiar that I almost believe you," she said, studying Maisie's face carefully.

"Yesterday you told us that you wanted to be a nurse," Felix said. "Like your aunt."

"My great-aunt, actually," Clara said. She began to unpack the basket, placing plates with slices of cold ham and thick-cut bread and cheese on the quilt. "She's a midwife in Maine, but it's so rural there that she does all kinds of medical work. She delivers babies and heals wounds and saves lives every day."

As Felix took this information in, he tried to imagine the connection between Clara's passion for healing and tending the sick and what lay ahead for her.

"Your great-aunt inspires you," Maisie surprised him by saying.

"She's a gift, I think. She's accomplished so many things, impacted so many lives, and is still alive to share those stories with me." Clara cut a piece of ham and took a bite. "Do you have someone like that in your life?"

Maisie thought of Great-Aunt Maisie, sitting in the nursing home. Every time they had visited, she'd tried to hug Maisie, but Maisie shrugged out of it. Her cloudy-blue eyes had struggled to make contact with Maisie's, and Maisie always looked away. When they'd visited just the other day, Great-Aunt Maisie had even tried to talk to Maisie about Elm Medona, and Maisie had dismissed her like she always did.

But thinking back on it now, it seemed that Great-Aunt Maisie had actually been trying to tell Maisie and Felix something.

"We have a great-aunt, too," Felix was saying. "She's old and sick, but when she was younger, she led a very interesting life, I think."

"Does she prefer not to talk about it?"

"No," Maisie said, "we prefer not to listen."

Clara's face changed. "Not listen?"

"Sitting here," Maisie said, "I'm thinking about her in her wheelchair, trying to talk to us, and I feel just awful."

"Well," Clara said, "it isn't too late, is it? When you get home you shall go directly to Great-Aunt—"

"Maisie," Maisie said. "I'm named for her."

"Great-Aunt Maisie," Clara said softly, clearly touched by this. "You will go to her and hear all the wonderful things she has to tell you."

"The last time we saw her," Felix said, "I had the strangest feeling that she wanted to tell us something important about Elm Medona."

"You didn't tell me that," Maisie said.

"What is Elm Medona?" asked Clara.

"Elm Medona," Felix said, "is the name of the house we live in. It's actually Great-Aunt Maisie's house."

"Oh! She lives with you!"

"No," Maisie said, "she lives in a hospital that takes care of her."

"Do you know that kind of tree, Clara?" Felix asked. "Elm Medona?"

Clara shook her head. "They don't grow here in Oxford."

Maisie slathered a piece of bread with butter and began to eat it. Felix could tell that her mind was working, trying to figure out all of these mysteries. Elm Medona and Dorence Atwater and, most of all, Clara Barton.

"Clara," Felix said.

She looked up and smiled her shy smile at him.

"We have something that we think belongs to you."

His eyes met Maisie's, and she nodded.

"Remember that paper we lost?"

"The one you found in the field?" Clara said. "I remember."

"Well . . ." He hesitated. How much should he say? What did he know, really? The letter would speak for itself. But what would Clara make of it when the Civil War was still years and years away? What would she make of the date almost three decades from now?

"What about the letter?" Clara said. "Is it a letter for me?"

"Yes," Maisie said firmly. "It is."

She reached over and took it from the place where Felix had laid it down, holding it out for Clara.

With a small but quizzical smile, Clara took it.

"How peculiar," she said.

That was the last thing Maisie and Felix heard Clara Barton say.

As soon as she said it, the air changed. A warm wind whipped around them. It smelled of everything good: cinnamon and Christmas trees and salty ocean air; fresh lemons and hot chocolate and a flower garden. It smelled like home.

Maisie gripped Felix's hand and held on tightly as they lifted and rolled.

"Clara!" Felix called. "Thank you!" But he wasn't at all certain that she heard him.

With a soft thud he landed facedown on the Oriental carpet in The Treasure Chest.

"We're back," Maisie said.

But Felix couldn't tell if she was glad or disappointed or simply as surprised as he was. He got to his feet and looked around the cluttered room. Everything seemed exactly as it had been when they entered.

"How did that happen?" Maisie asked.

"Beats me."

"We weren't holding the letter," Maisie said,

thinking out loud. "Clara was."

"Do you think that's what sent us back? Giving it to Clara?"

"Maybe," Maisie said.

"I'm sorry," Felix said. "I know you weren't ready to leave."

"After we read the letter," she said, "I didn't really want to stick around. All those dead soldiers. The war coming. At least here I don't know what to expect, and that feels a whole lot better."

"Poor Clara," Felix said.

"No," Maisie said. "She's going to help all of those families. She's going to make a difference."

Felix thought about that. "I guess you're right," he said thoughtfully.

Early morning light was just beginning to illuminate the ornate stained-glass window, casting beautiful rays of color into The Treasure Chest. Felix walked slowly to the window, his hand gently brushing items as he passed the desk and then a table, both of them covered with strange and commonplace items. *Could each of these things take us into the past and reveal their secrets to us?* Felix wondered. As his fingertips grazed tiny silken shoes, a test tube, a quill pen, and a geode, his body tingled with curiosity.

At the window, he gazed down at the sight of his

mother's Mustang parked in the driveway.

"Well," he said, "Mom's home."

"Mom," Maisie said as if the impact of their absence had just hit her. "Uh-oh."

Felix grimaced. "I guess we'd better go upstairs and take our punishment."

Reluctantly, Maisie agreed.

They left The Treasure Chest, both of them glancing over their shoulders at it as they walked away, until even those backward glances no longer offered a glimpse of it. Down the stairs, they touched the wall, slowly rotating it back in place and hiding the secret entrance to The Treasure Chest again.

On their way down the Grand Staircase, Maisie paused at the photograph of Great-Aunt Maisie as a young girl.

"What are you up to?" Maisie whispered to her.

Then she continued down the staircase, across the Grand Ballroom, and into the Dining Room. She turned the knob on the door that led to the servants' stairway, but it didn't budge.

"Locked!" she cried.

Felix looked under the rug for the key, but it was gone.

"Now what?" asked Maisie.

"The dumbwaiter?" Maisie offered.

"We can't just pop out of the dumbwaiter after having been missing all this time. Mom will have a heart attack."

"And who knows who's up there with her, probably making those flyers like they hang up for missing kids," Maisie agreed.

For a moment, Felix actually felt excited. "Do you think Dad flew here from Qatar? He must have come to help Mom find us."

Despite her own excitement at the idea, Maisie said, "But you're right. We still can't pop out of the dumbwaiter like that. How will we explain why we were in here in the first place?"

"There must be another way in," Felix said, thinking hard.

Maisie groaned. "If we get caught in here, we are going to get into the worst trouble of our lives."

"There's that," Felix said.

Then he remembered something the Woman in Pink had told them. There was an entrance to the Kitchen that was hidden from view so that guests would not see delivery vehicles or servants enter the house. She'd said it was still used for deliveries today. That might be just the right way to exit.

"Come on," Felix said, tugging his sister's Mets fleece. "We've got to get to the cottage's Kitchen."

He led her down the steps in the Dining Room

to the Kitchen. Then they took the short flight
of stairs down to the subbasement where the little
train brought the coal in from the hidden tunnel.
They navigated through the winding tunnel,
passing wine cellars and storage spaces until they
saw a glimmer of light from a high, small window.

"Remember the entrance hidden by . . . how
did the docent describe it? A portico and foliage?"
Felix said, pleased he'd remembered the new word.

"Uh . . . no," Maisie admitted.

"Well, good thing one of us listened to the
tour," Felix grinned. "There's a door over here that
people on the inside can open, but people on the
outside can't."

Sure enough, a very ordinary-looking door
painted a dull red stood right under the small
window. Felix turned the knob, and it opened as
easily as that. A blast of hot air hit him in the face.

They stepped outside onto the circular drive
under an arbor of purple wisteria so heavy it
obscured where they stood. By the time they walked
around the house to the side entrance that led to
their apartment, they were drenched in sweat.

"Sitting with Clara at lunch," Maisie said,
"I promised myself not to complain so much at
home, but I'm already breaking that promise. It's
still hot and miserable here."

Felix stopped at the door and looked at Maisie, puzzled.

"What's wrong?" she said.

"You're right. We were at lunch with Clara, but here we are now, and it's morning."

"Do you think we traveled a whole day and night to get back?" she asked.

Felix shrugged. "Maybe."

Maisie took a deep breath and opened the door. "Here we go," she said.

Slowly, they climbed the stairs to the apartment, afraid of what would happen when they opened the door.

They were not at all prepared for what they found.

The kitchen looked exactly as they had left it. Even the dirty dinner dishes with the orange remnants of mac and cheese had not been cleared.

Before they had a chance to comment on any of it, their mother stumbled into the kitchen, yawning, her hair all tangled from sleeping on it, and her face creased from lying on her pillow.

When she saw them standing there, she frowned. "You're up already?"

Maisie and Felix glanced at each other.

"Why are you just standing there like that?" she said suspiciously.

Once again, they glanced at each other.

"Okay, fess up. What have you done?" she demanded.

When they didn't answer, she muttered, "I don't like surprises before I've even had my first cup of coffee."

With that, she went over to the coffeemaker and busied herself measuring grounds and filling it with water. She pressed the BREW button and turned back to them.

"Mom," Felix finally managed to say, "what day is it?"

"Thursday," she said.

"Thursday, September . . . ?"

"Fifth," she said, narrowing her eyes.

Now Maisie and Felix exchanged stunned looks. They had traveled to 1836, spent a night at Captain Stephen Barton's farm in Oxford, Massachusetts, and spent another half day with Clara there, yet apparently no time had passed at all.

"Amazing," Maisie whispered.

"It's like we didn't leave at all," Felix said.

Their mother poured coffee into her SAIL NEWPORT mug that had come in the preservation society's gift basket when they moved in. She studied both of them as she took a big swallow.

Then she pointed her finger and said,

"September fifth. You know what today is."

Felix groaned. "School."

Their mother smiled. "School. I'm going to shower, and you two need to get ready."

"Mom?" Maisie called to her back.

Their mother poked her head around the doorway.

"Could we go visit Great-Aunt Maisie after school?"

With that, their mother came all the way back into the kitchen.

"*You* want to visit *Great-Aunt Maisie*?"

Maisie nodded.

Their mother dramatically placed the back of her hand onto Maisie's forehead, then Felix's. "No fever," she said. "Maybe heat exhaustion?" Shaking her head, she walked back out.

In no time, they heard the sound of the shower and their mother humming some show tune.

In a way, everything was perfectly normal. And in another way, nothing at all was the same.

· CHAPTER THIRTEEN ·

◦ The First Day of School ◦

"I'm sorry, Mrs. Robbins," Vice Principal Gale said, "but it's school policy to separate twins."

Vice Principal Gale looked like a tank. Short and stout, she seemed as tall as she was wide, and her skirt and her matching jacket were army green. Adding to the overall military impression she made, her voice rat-a-tatted like a machine gun. She didn't sound at all sorry that Maisie and Felix had been placed in different fifth-grade classrooms.

"Mrs. Gale," their mother said, speaking in a hushed tone. "I understand the policy, I do. But Maisie and Felix have had such a disruptive year, with their father and I divorcing and him taking a job far away, and then being uprooted, leaving our home, and moving here to Newport." Her voice cracked. All of this upheaval had taken its toll on her, too.

Mrs. Gale nodded with a sharp bend of her chin. "I understand. That is a lot of disruption, you're absolutely right."

Maisie and Felix sighed with relief.

"However, a policy is a policy. And I have found children to be remarkably resilient."

"What?" their mother said.

"So Maisie here will be in Mrs. Witherspoon's class," Mrs. Gale said, placing a firm hand on Maisie's shoulder, "and Felix will be in Miss Landers's." She placed her other hand squarely on Felix's shoulder.

"But, Mrs. Gale—" their mother began.

Mrs. Gale had already begun to move them down the corridor, her hands on their shoulders, keeping a tight grip.

"Kids?" their mother called after them.

But so firm was Mrs. Gale's grip that they couldn't turn their heads or even lift their arms to wave good-bye.

P.S. 3, their school in New York, had been a low, modern building built in the early 1960s. It had scuffed linoleum floors in varying patterns of faded green and gold, faded yellow and green, and faded brown and gold. The walls were painted a dingy mustard, and the fluorescent lights emitted a constant hum throughout the day.

But this school was old and well-kempt, with polished wooden floors and metal pegs to hang coats and fancy molding around the tops of the walls. The walls themselves were half paneled, then painted a buttery yellow all the way up to those fancy moldings. The school smelled as if someone had just gone through it and polished every inch of it with lemon furniture wax and then added a hint of wool and some chalk dust.

Despite himself, Felix fell in love with the school as Mrs. Gale propelled him toward Miss Landers's classroom. Maisie, however, looked miserable. She'd spent way too much time trying to figure out what to wear. Jeans or a skirt? Sneakers or flip-flops? A T-shirt or a button-down shirt? Finally, exasperated, Felix had told her to dress however she would dress back at P.S. 3. But now she wondered if her pink Converse high tops, the jean skirt she'd made herself from an old pair of her mother's Levi's, and the faded green T-shirt that said STRAWBERRY FIELDS FOREVER were the right choice.

"Maisie," Mrs. Gale said, stopping them from going

any farther, "this is Mrs. Witherspoon's classroom."

Mrs. Gale dropped her hand from Felix's shoulder and ordered him to wait in the corridor. Felix watched as his sister, shoulders slumped, scuffled in behind the vice principal.

With a quick handover of permanent records and grade transcripts, Mrs. Gale was gone, and Maisie was left standing awkwardly in front of a classroom of twenty-eight students, all of them staring at her. The meeting with the vice principal had taken longer than expected, and Felix and Maisie would be walking into their classrooms after they had already started.

Mrs. Witherspoon was old and wrinkly with a gray bun and glasses that made her eyes look huge and buggy.

"So . . . ," she said, scanning the folders. "Maisie?"

Maisie nodded.

"Like the department store?" someone in the back heckled.

"No," Maisie said at the exact time that Mrs. Witherspoon said, "Yes."

"No," Maisie said again, louder this time. "That's Ma-cy."

"Well, excuse me," the heckler said. He was a tall boy with a sweep of bangs over his forehead and a jersey with a number on it.

The class laughed.

"All right, Maisie," Mrs. Witherspoon continued. "There's a seat for you right up front." She handed Maisie a stack of textbooks and then seemed to forget all about her.

"Back to our math review," Mrs. Witherspoon said.

She went up to the blackboard and began to write problems on the board. Maisie glanced around. Some kids were copying the problems into notebooks, some were whispering to one another, and some were simply daydreaming. It seemed like Maisie was already forgotten.

She took a pencil and a notebook from her backpack and sighed. Now she knew which kind of new kid she was: the kind who simply disappeared.

Miss Landers was beautiful. She had long, dark hair and big, blue eyes, like Snow White come to life. She gushed over Felix, telling him how she had lived in New York City during college.

"Boys and girls," she said, "isn't New York City an exciting place? What do we know about it?"

She pulled a map down over the blackboard. First she pointed out Newport, then New York state, then New York City.

Kids shouted out things they knew about it, like Broadway and the ball dropping in Times Square on New Year's Eve and the Metropolitan Museum of Art.

"Yes! Yes!" Miss Landers cried after each new thing, which she then wrote on the blackboard in lovely, curly penmanship. "We'll add *From the Mixed-Up Files of Mrs. Basil E. Frankweiler* to our reading list this year. The story takes place in New York City," she said as she wrote the book's title on the board, too.

"Aren't we lucky to have Felix in our classroom? He can tell us so many things about New York City. Maybe we'll do a project on New York City."

Excitement bubbled up in the room as Miss Landers went on and on about New York City, and kids asked Felix if he'd ever been to the Thanksgiving Day parade and if he'd lived in an apartment and if he took the subway alone.

"Now," Miss Landers said after a good, long while, "who can find a seat for Felix?"

Children stood and reshuffled themselves, calling, "Sit here, Felix, sit here!"

Grinning, Felix made his way down the aisle to a seat smack in the middle of everybody and sat down.

In Mrs. Witherspoon's classroom, things weren't going as well.

"For your first homework assignment, you must write a report on someone who changed the world," Mrs. Witherspoon said.

"Like Lance Armstrong?" Ginger Beatty said.

Mrs. Witherspoon frowned. "Lance Armstrong . . . Lance Armstrong . . ."

"Come on, Mrs. W," Patrick Sullivan groaned. "He's like the most famous cyclist ever."

"And he survived cancer," Ginger added primly.

"Oh, yes," Mrs. Witherspoon said. "The yellow rubber bands."

"Livestrong bracelets," Ginger corrected.

Mrs. Witherspoon nodded. "Well, actually, Mr. Armstrong does not qualify for this report. You'll need to pick a person who isn't widely known, yet changed history."

The class waited for her to say more, but Mrs. Witherspoon just sighed and glanced at the clock.

"Shall we line up for dismissal?" she said.

"But how many pages do we have to write?" Molly Tapper cried. All day long Molly had whined and gotten nervous about almost everything. "And when is it due?"

"The report is going to be oral. You'll stand right up here in the front of the classroom and give the report. On Monday."

The whole class seemed to groan at once.

"Is Abraham Lincoln okay?" Thad Brown asked. Thad was taller and older than everyone else. Maisie wondered if he'd already started to shave or if he just had kind of a grimy chin.

"No, no," Mrs. Witherspoon said. "Everyone in this classroom has heard of Abraham Lincoln."

Maisie wanted to ask if they had to give a report on somebody no one had ever heard of, how were they supposed to pick someone to write about. But she didn't want to draw attention to herself. She'd managed to pass the whole day without one person talking to her. On her way to recess, she'd passed Felix, and he was so busy talking to a bunch of kids, he didn't even notice her.

She waited until it was her row's turn to get in line. Then she collected her things from her cubby and stood in the dismissal line. Molly Tapper stood next to her.

"I don't know who to write this report on," Molly said to her in a trembling voice.

"You'll think of somebody," Maisie said.

"How?"

Maisie shrugged.

Mrs. Witherspoon clapped her hands to get the class's attention.

"By the way, you are not allowed to use the

computer for this assignment. No Google or Wahoo."

The class tittered.

"Yahoo," someone said.

"Or that," Mrs. Witherspoon said.

"But how will we get our information?" Molly said.

"Go to the library," Mrs. Witherspoon said.

"The *library*?" Molly whined.

"Yes," Mrs. Witherspoon said, clearly finished with the discussion and the kids. "The library."

The dismissal bell rang.

"And I don't know if my mother will even take me to the library . . ."

Molly's voice droned on and on, high-pitched and shrill. Slowly, the line began to inch forward.

The weight of all the things in her life made Maisie move heavily. How would she ever survive the school year? How would she ever even write this report? Then, as clear as anything, a brilliant idea came to her. The most brilliant idea. She practically smiled at poor Molly Tapper . . . she practically smiled at old Mrs. Witherspoon, standing there all flustered as the class filed out. . . she practically smiled at Newport, Rhode Island, waiting right out the big double doors.

Because Maisie knew absolutely who she would write about.

·CHAPTER FOURTEEN·

Angel of the Battlefield

"I have the worst teacher ever!" Maisie told Felix outside the school. "She's ancient."

"Oooh," Felix said. "Sorry."

They walked along the broad street, past the small shops and cafés that lined it. The cool air already hinted at autumn, and Felix could see splashes of color as the leaves on the trees were just beginning to turn red and gold. If they turned right onto Thames Street, they could walk along the harbor. It wasn't the direct way home, but Felix wanted to look at the boats there, the sleek yachts with exotic locations and the sailboats with their mysterious names. The sailors intrigued him, too. They had weathered faces and strong arms, and a look about them like they'd led interesting lives. Felix liked to try and imagine what it might be like to sail across the ocean.

Just when he was about to suggest going that way, Maisie grabbed his arm and tugged him in the opposite direction.

"But Mrs. Witherspoon gave us the most wonderful assignment ever," Maisie said.

"Since when does homework make you happy?" Felix said.

"The assignment is on someone who changed history, someone most people haven't heard of."

Felix nodded. "Like Clara Barton?" he said.

"Who knows? Maybe that letter from Dorence Atwater influenced history," Maisie said.

"And in there is the answer," Maisie said, pointing to the library.

They climbed the stairs and walked inside. Maisie marched right up to the information desk.

"I'm looking for information on someone named Clara Barton, please. And my teacher said we couldn't use the Internet."

The librarian smiled. "Oh, you have Mrs. Witherspoon, I see." The librarian tapped on her computer keyboard, then said, "Right this way."

Maisie and Felix followed the librarian up the stairs and through a maze of rows and rows of books, until she finally stopped, scanned the shelves, and then pointed.

"This row," she said with a sweep of her hand.

"You mean the book's on this shelf?" asked Maisie.

"No," answered the librarian with a grin. "*All* the books on that shelf are about Clara Barton."

"Wow," Felix said under his breath.

Felix and Maisie lifted their gaze to take in all the books with the name CLARA BARTON on their spines.

"If you need anything else, come get me," the librarian said.

When she walked away, Maisie and Felix looked from the books on the shelf to each other and then back to the books.

"I guess," Maisie said finally, "she did something important. Maybe she became the first woman doctor." Her voice sounded hushed and awed as if just the sight of these books had great significance. "Or the first woman general in the army."

"She would have liked that," Felix said.

"I guess there's enough here for my report," Maisie said, still staring up at the books without taking even one of them down from its place on the shelf.

"I guess," Felix said.

Maisie slowly reached a hand up and took one

of the books. The picture on the cover showed a stern-faced woman with dark hair beneath a cap.

"Is that Clara?" Felix asked, surprised.

Maisie nodded.

Once on television he'd seen some device that could take a picture of a baby and age it so that you could see that person as a child and then a teenager and then older and older, all the way through old age. That's what he felt he was looking at. No matter how hard he stared, he could not find the teenage Clara in this middle-aged woman's face.

Maisie flipped the book open and randomly stopped on a page.

"'On April 20, 1862, after the First Battle of Bull Run, General William Hammond gave Clara Barton permission to ride in army ambulances. There, she provided comfort and nursing to the soldiers,'" she read. "'She petitioned to bring her own medical supplies . . . in July 1862, she traveled behind the lines to some of the grimmest battlefields of the war, including the Siege of Petersburg and Richmond, Virginia.'"

"She did it," Felix said. "She went to war, in a way."

"In the best way a woman could back in 1862, I guess," Maisie said thoughtfully. "'Eventually,'" Maisie read, "'she was put in charge of all the hospitals.'"

Now Felix took one of the books from the shelf. He went to the index in the back and looked for Dorence Atwater. When he found it, he turned to that page and read to himself about the very list he and Maisie had held in their hands.

"Listen to this," Felix said. "Abraham Lincoln put her in charge of finding out all of the names of the men from the Union Army who were missing and contacting those families!"

Maisie had now filled her arms with Clara Barton books. She held one up for Felix to see.

He read its title: *Clara Barton: Founder of the American Red Cross.*

The enormity of what he and Maisie had experienced filled him.

"The Red Cross," Felix managed to say. "That's who helps during hurricanes and tornadoes and fires and—"

"Wars," Maisie added.

She took her brother's hand, awkwardly with all the books she held, and squeezed it. They had been through so much together, the two of them. Not just skinned knees and bad dreams, but their parents' divorce and moving from the city to this new, unfamiliar place. And then their trip to The Treasure Chest that sent them back in time.

They stood like that, hand in hand, the books

about Clara Barton between them. Felix didn't say anything. He was too busy wondering where else The Treasure Chest might bring them. Was it possible that they could control it somehow and get back to earlier this very year? To their room on Bethune Street when their parents were still married and their family was still together?

"You were right, Felix," Maisie said softly. "This isn't something we should mess with. One time-travel trip per lifetime is enough."

"What if . . . ," Felix began.

But in her typical fashion, Maisie had moved on, dropping his hand and heading back downstairs to check out the books.

Maybe that was just as well, he decided. There were too many what-ifs. At least for now.

At night, Island Retirement Center seemed like a haunted house, all shadows and dim lights, strange moans and empty hallways. Even the nurses' station was deserted, and the television in the solarium was turned down so low it seemed to be whispering. Maisie and Felix and their mother practically tiptoed to Great-Aunt Maisie's room.

They found the door open, and Great-Aunt Maisie propped up in bed with lots of pillows behind

her and around her as if the pillows actually kept her
upright. Her bedside table had a vase of fresh peonies.
Her lips had their characteristic Chanel Red lipstick
on them. Her hair had been tied back in a neat little
bun. When they walked into the room, she smiled her
crooked smile.

"What a lovely surprise," she said.

Their mother sat beside her on the bed. "The
children insisted on visiting, darling," she told
Great-Aunt Maisie. "They said they wanted to
see you."

Great-Aunt Maisie patted their mother's hand.
"Actually, dear, I want to see the children as well."

Maisie went to the other side of the bed and
took Great-Aunt Maisie's hand in her own. She
ignored her mother's surprised face and focused
on her aunt instead.

"Why don't you rustle up some ginger ale for your
old aunt?" Great-Aunt Maisie said to their mother.

"Great-Aunt Maisie," she said, "you sound a little
better. Your words, I mean. They're clearer than
before."

Felix had noticed that, too, and he nodded when
his mother said it. "I can understand you almost
perfectly," he added.

Great-Aunt Maisie smiled. "No ice, dear," she said.

Once their mother had gone, Felix joined

Maisie at their great-aunt's bedside.

"Tell me," Great-Aunt Maisie said. "How is my home? How is Elm Medona?"

"It's fine," Felix answered politely.

"The apartment is hot and stuffy," Maisie said. "It's cramped, too, and feels like a prison."

Great-Aunt Maisie laughed. "I agree," she said. "I spent many a lonely night up there."

Felix said, "It's not so bad."

"You're just like my brother, Thorne," Great-Aunt Maisie said, delighted. "Always optimistic. Always polite." She wagged a finger at Felix. "But Thorne had a dark side, too." Then she turned her blue eyes onto Maisie. "But how is the cottage itself?"

"Well," Maisie said carefully, trying to decide how much to say. "We only got to go inside once."

"Officially," Felix said.

Great-Aunt Maisie waited.

"Please don't tell," Maisie said in a rush of words, "but we did sneak back in once . . . or twice."

Their great-aunt broke into a grin. "I thought you might! Marvelous!"

"The room they call The Treasure Chest . . . ," Maisie began.

"Yes?" Great-Aunt Maisie said.

"We went in there the other day, and something

very strange happened."

Great-Aunt Maisie's grin widened. "Yes?" she said again, even more eagerly this time.

"We found a letter, and it seemed like when we held it, we were able to—"

"One ginger ale," their mother announced, walking in with a plastic cup full of soda. "No ice."

Great-Aunt Maisie let out a sigh.

"You did say no ice, didn't you?" their mother said.

"Oh, it's not that," Great-Aunt Maisie said.

"Since you're feeling so well," their mother said, "how about a game of hearts?"

"That's a fine idea," their great-aunt said.

Great-Aunt Maisie shot the moon four consecutive times, ending the game in twenty minutes flat. She thanked them for coming and asked if they would visit again soon.

First their mother, then Felix, then Maisie kissed Great-Aunt Maisie's forehead and prepared to leave.

"Maisie," Great-Aunt Maisie said, stopping her at the door. "What was the name?"

Maisie squinted, trying to figure out what Great-Aunt Maisie meant.

Great-Aunt Maisie looked at her hopefully. "Just tell me who you met. Please."

"Clara Barton," Maisie said in a near whisper.

Great-Aunt Maisie smiled and rested her head against her throne of pillows. "Clara Barton," she said, satisfied.

Their mother appeared again at the doorway. "Don't bother her with that report of yours, Maisie. Let her get some sleep."

But Maisie stayed put, watching her great-aunt gently drift off to sleep, a slight smile on her red lipsticked lips.

Over the next days, school went as school does. There were secrets whispered, feelings hurt; homework given, math explained. Outside the classroom windows, more and more leaves turned from green to red and yellow. The air took on a chill, especially at night and first thing in the morning. Maisie and Felix's mother worked long hours at the law office, and they made themselves dinners of scrambled eggs or bologna sandwiches. With each passing day, Maisie hated Mrs. Witherspoon more, and Felix loved Miss Landers even more.

"You know," Maisie said as Felix washed the dishes from their dinner one Friday night, "I think that whole experience was for us to get to

know Great-Aunt Maisie. To maybe learn from
her the way Clara learned from her great-aunt."

Felix paused, then said quietly, "I want to go back."

"Back to the Barton farm?" Maisie said.

He shook his head.

"You mean you want to go back to The Treasure
Chest?" Maisie asked, surprised.

"I've thought about it, and yes, I want to try
again."

"No way," Maisie said firmly.

"But you wanted to—"

"I did. But it's too scary. Too unpredictable.
We got back by accident this time. What if we got
stuck next time? What if we weren't in a place as
lovely as the Barton farm?"

"Oh, Maisie, we can't just stay cooped up here
all the time," Felix said.

Maisie looked at her brother as if he were a
stranger. The boy who had to sleep with a light on,
who couldn't even watch mildly scary movies, was
suddenly willing to go back to The Treasure Chest
and go anywhere at all.

"I don't know," she said. "We could land in a
war or a dungeon or—"

"Or at 10 Bethune Street," he blurted. "Or
earlier this year."

Maisie let the wonderful idea sink in. "Do you

think we can? Really?"

Felix shrugged. "I don't know. But it's worth a try, isn't it?"

Maisie did not have to consider his proposition for too long.

"I suppose if we made it happen once, we might be able to do it again," she said.

"This time, we have to think as hard as we can about New York City and our street. We have to concentrate all of our energy on that."

Far below, they could hear the downstairs door open and then close, signaling that their mother was home from work.

"All right," Maisie said. "I'm in."

Felix extended his hand, and Maisie took it.

"Tomorrow night?" Felix asked.

Their mother's footsteps clomped up the stairs.

Maisie nodded. "To tomorrow," she said.

"To yesterday," Felix said.

Their mother's key jiggled in the lock. The door creaked open, and she walked in, tired and wrinkled. She paused, her key still in her hand, and studied them.

"Are you two up to something?" she asked.

Maisie and Felix shrugged.

"Who, us?" Maisie said.

Already they could see their old familiar street

with the playground at one end and the Hudson
River at the other, with the smell of the Laundromat
mixing with Chinese food and exhaust hanging in
the air, with their mother and father singing in the
kitchen, and a whole world of happy possibilities
right out the door waiting for them.

CLARA BARTON
December 25, 1821–April 12, 1912

Clara Barton was born Clarissa Harlowe Barton on Christmas Day, 1821, in Oxford, Massachusetts. She was the fifth and youngest child of Captain Stephen Barton and Sarah Stone Barton. Clara's father was a farmer and horse breeder, and it was his military stories about fighting in several Indian wars that inspired her patriotism, love of history, and, ultimately, her desire to aid wounded soldiers.

Clara's immediate family played an important role in her education. Clara's older sisters, Dolly and Sally, taught her to read at a very young age. Her brother Stephen tutored her in math, and her brother David taught her to horseback ride when she was five years old. But things changed in the Barton family when Clara was eleven. David fell from the rafters of a barn and was seriously injured. Clara dedicated herself to nursing him day and night for over two years.

Despite showing a talent for caring for the sick, Clara's parents urged her to pursue a career as a teacher. She taught in a school for ten years and eventually moved to Bordentown, New Jersey, where she started a free public school. The school was so successful that a new building was constructed and more teachers were hired. However, when the school hired a man as headmaster at a salary higher than Clara's, Clara demanded equal pay. The school refused to pay a woman the same salary that a man would get, so Clara resigned and took a new job in Washington, D.C.

In Washington, D.C., Clara was the first woman clerk hired in the patent office, and she earned the same salary as a man. Now Clara was more motivated than ever to help women obtain jobs—especially in government services—and equal pay. It was around this time that she first became known as a pioneer for women's rights.

On April 19, 1861, a week after the Civil War began, troops from the Sixth Massachusetts regiment arrived in Washington. Clara went to the train station to meet the men, some of whom she had taught when they were schoolboys. The city was so crowded with other troops that the soldiers were sent to the Capitol building. But Clara took the most seriously wounded to her sister Sally's house and nursed them. She also gathered clothing, food, and other supplies for the soldiers from local merchants. Later in her life, she credited her father's own war stories and his patriotism with her desire to help the Civil War soldiers.

In 1861, Washington, D.C., became filled with wounded soldiers after a particularly bloody battle near Manassas, Virginia. Clara cared for the wounded, but soon she realized that the place she was most needed was the battlefield. She petitioned the government and leaders in the army and was allowed to take her wagons filled with supplies through the lines. She arrived at Culpeper, Virginia, two days after a fierce battle and immediately set to work at a poorly equipped field hospital. For two days and two nights, Clara tended the wounded soldiers.

These experiences with wounded soldiers confirmed her belief that she was needed on the battlefields—not back in Washington, D.C. She lobbied the Senate relentlessly for more supplies and better field hospitals, all the while nursing the wounded at major battles such as Antietam and Fredericksburg.

In 1865, after the Civil War ended, President Lincoln put Clara in charge of locating missing prisoners of war. She and her assistants answered thousands of letters that poured in, giving or requesting information about the dead and missing.

Around this time, a young Union soldier named Dorence Atwater came to Clara's door. While being held by the Confederates in a South Carolina prisoner of war camp, Dorence copied down an enormous list of dead soldiers' names. When Dorence was released from prison, he hid this list in a laundry bag and smuggled it through enemy lines. Afraid that the names of the men who had died would never get to their families, he asked Clara Barton to help him publish the list and find the families of the soldiers. She agreed. His list of nearly thirteen thousand men, later called "The Atwater List," became famous and helped thousands of families learn the fate of their loved ones.

While Clara was on a vacation in Europe in 1870, the Franco-Prussian war broke out. She heard about the newly established International Committee of the Red Cross—a relief organization to help nurse wounded soldiers—and offered her services to them. Throughout the war, Clara set up aid centers in several war-torn cities and was awarded the Iron Cross, a special military honor.

Clara Barton began her campaign for an American Red Cross in 1873; however, she met resistance. Most Americans thought this organization was unnecessary since they could not imagine that the United States would ever again face a war as terrible as the Civil War. But Clara convinced President James Garfield that the new American Red Cross could respond to crises other than war. In 1882, that dream came true. Over the next two decades, Clara and the American Red Cross provided nurses, basic supplies, and aid centers in emergencies as varied as forest fires, floods, and outbreaks of typhoid and yellow fever.

The last contribution Clara Barton made to the American Red Cross was in September 1900. After the devastating hurricane and tidal wave that hit Galveston, Texas, and killed six thousand people, Clara established an orphanage. She also helped obtain the materials needed to rebuild houses and organized newspapers across the country to accept contributions on behalf of the relief effort.

Clara Barton was a pioneer in the field of nursing. She is famous as the founder of the American Red Cross. But she is perhaps most beloved for her role on the battlefields of the Civil War, where she earned the love and respect of thousands and became known as the Angel of the Battlefield.

— THE —

TREASURE
·CHEST·E

No. 2 *Little Lion*

Felix landed with a splash. He opened his eyes and saw that he was underwater. Not just any water, either. This water was so clear that he could see Maisie's legs thrashing; a school of bright, yellow fish swimming past; and the soft, sandy bottom way, way beneath him. He swam upward, kicking his legs hard until he reached the surface. When his head finally popped out of the water, he took a big, deep breath and looked around. In the distance lay a white sand beach fringed with palm trees. But all around him Felix saw nothing but beautiful turquoise water. Until Maisie appeared—sputtering and shaking the water from her hair, with the coin pressed firmly in her fist.

"Over here!" Felix called, waving to her. He had certainly not expected this. Not at all. They were in the ocean!

Maisie looked about as angry as she could look. Felix watched her dive into the water and swim purposefully toward him. She was a good swimmer. And so was he. They had learned to swim when they were five at the Carmine Street Pool and tied for first place in a relay race there when they were seven.

The sun shone bright and warm above them. Felix lay on his back and floated gently, gazing up at the clear, blue sky.

When Maisie reached him, she treaded water beside him.

"This," she said, "is not New York."

Felix smiled. "Nope," he said.

"This is all your fault," she said. "If you'd just let me find those blueprints, we wouldn't be in the middle of the ocean right now."

"First of all, we're not in the middle of the ocean. The beach is right over there. Second of all, this is actually kind of nice."

Maisie sighed. Clearly her brother was not going to be any help figuring out where they'd landed. Or why. She took a breath, stretched out her arms, and began to swim.

"Hey! Where are you going?" Felix called after her.

"To shore!" Maisie yelled back. And then she kept on swimming.